HANGING BY A THREAD . . .

Outside the mob was growing louder, rowdier. They were a pack of dogs who had tasted blood and were thirsty for more. In the tangle of words pouring from them I heard eager talk of hanging.

I rolled over and groaned. Right then I could have killed Fiddler Smith with my own hands, for this was his fault entirely.

Part of me wanted to pound on the shed door and shout out that the man who really deserved to hang was Fiddler Smith, not me. It was Fiddler who had actually done the deed, Fiddler who had left me helpless, to be found and charged the price of a crime that had not been mine.

A fierce defiance sparked in me. No. I wouldn't stand by, waiting for a gaggle of drunks to end my life. I would fight to the end—no, until the end was avoided . . .

ST. MARTIN'S PAPERBACKS TITLES
BY CAMERON JUDD

THE GLORY RIVER
SNOW SKY
CORRIGAN
TIMBER CREEK
TEXAS FREEDOM
RENEGADE LAWMEN

RENEGADE LAWMEN

(previously published as
Fiddler and McCan)

CAMERON JUDD

St. Martin's Paperbacks

Renegade Lawmen was previously published under the title *Fiddler and McCan*.

RENEGADE LAWMEN

Copyright © 1992 by Cameron Judd.

ISBN: 0-312-96896-5

Printed in the United States of America

Bantam Domain edition / December 1992
St. Martin's Paperbacks edition / March 1999

10 9 8 7 6 5 4 3 2 1

For Joan, who kept asking:
"Whatever happened to
Luke McCan?"

RENEGADE LAWMEN

PART ONE

WALDEN CITY

Chapter 1

It was hard to know who to side with: the skinny fiddle player with the missing ear or the hefty trail bum with the harelip. The former was taking some fierce punishment from the latter, but then, he had brought it on himself by his heartless teasing. I am a man with little sympathy for anyone who taunts another because of his looks, for there's not a one of us who can control what nature gives us, or fails to.

Of course, I couldn't stand by and see a small man beaten to death by a big one, either, no matter what the circumstances. That made my decision for me. I hefted up a big cuspidor, advanced, and brought it down as hard as I could on the back of the bigger man's head. It made for quite a messy explosion.

I had hoped it would drop him. It didn't. He turned and glared at me in disbelief, stinking cuspidor muck running all down both sides of his wide head. He had eyes that drilled like augers. His nose was wide and flat, like his face; his whiskers were as coarse as wool and thirstily soaking up the foul stuff I had just baptized him with.

The whiskers hid his mouth deformity fairly well, but his speech betrayed it. I couldn't make out all he said—mostly just catch cusswords that came out with their edges rounded off. His general point came through even if his words didn't, that being that I had been mighty foolish to cut into his business in so rude a manner.

His partner had been holding the fiddler from behind during the beating. He gave me the ugliest, most threatening grin I had ever received. He was a shrimpy man with a beard worthy of Elijah; his eyes were bright with the prophecy of my impending doomsday.

The fiddler was the only one who welcomed my intrusion. He took advantage of the distraction to wriggle free and dance off, very spritely, to the corner. From there he poked fun at his interrupted tormentors, obviously having gained no wisdom from suffering.

I felt surges of both anger and fear. I had butted into this situation only because I had thought that the fiddle player was about to be killed, for he had howled pitifully at every blow he took. Yet now it seemed he hadn't been hurt at all—in other words, I had endangered myself for darn little reason. That accounted for my anger. The fact that the harelipped man was big enough to single-handedly separate me from my limbs accounted for my fear.

"Have yourself some tobacco, rabbit-mouth, have yourself a chew!" the fiddle player chortled from his safe distance. His fiddle and bow lay at his feet, kicked into the corner earlier by the two hardcases. The fiddler stooped and snatched them up. The rosiny bow dragged across the strings and made a high, scratchy drone that melted into music. The fiddler's voice rang out, shouting more than singing in raucous jubilee—"Well, I went down in Helltown, to see that devil chain down . . ."

Now I knew how the Romans felt as Nero fiddled while their world crumbled to ash around them.

The hardcases advanced and I backed up, promising myself that if I lived to get out of this place I'd never lend a hand to any more one-eared fiddlers for the rest of my days.

"Here now, let's have no more trouble!" pleaded the wiry barkeep from behind his protecting counter. He had been yelping and begging for peace throughout the whole thing.

The harelipped man said something to me that I couldn't understand. Elijah the Prophet interpreted: "Peahead says he's going to pluck out them curls of yours like the feathers of a roasting hen."

Meanwhile, the exuberant fiddler was scratching and shouting away, ". . . Johnny, won't you ramble? Hoe, hoe, hoe . . ."

I wanted to ramble myself, not that there was any way with these two between me and the door. If the side window had been open I would have made a dive out of it, but it wasn't open, for outside the February cold still crawled over the western Nebraska landscape.

"Listen, friend, you've got my apology," I said placatingly. "I thought you were getting a little rough on the fiddler, that's all."

Another muffled statement, another interpretation: "Peahead says the fiddler made fun of his mouth. Peahead don't stand for nobody making fun of his mouth."

"I don't blame you, Peahead, I don't blame you at all," I replied. "He had no right to tease you. Listen, I'm mighty sorry about the cuspidor. I'll pay right out of my own pocket for a bath for you, I promise."

The white-bearded one shook his head. "You shouldn't have called him Peahead. Peahead don't like nobody but his friends calling him that."

"Peahead!" yelled the fiddler at once, having heard the last statement. His fiddle droned up high like an excited bee. "Well, I went down in Helltown, to see old Peahead chain down! Peahead, won't you ramble, hoe, hoe, harelip!"

"Here now, don't do that," the barkeep said feebly.

The fiddler's mockery proved helpful to me this time, for it snatched the attention of Peahead and his partner away from me for a moment. In that moment I balled up my fists and lunged forward, striking two blows in tandem, the first pounding into Peahead, the second into his companion.

The effort jolted me worse than my victims. These fellows were solid, even the little one. My attack did no more than draw their attention back my way.

"Fiddle man!" I yelled, backing up again, wishing my gunbelt was hanging around me, not that wall peg behind the bar. "Fiddle man, this is your fight, not mine! Get over here and help me!"

". . . Peahead, won't you ramble? Hoe, hoe, hoe!" He was so caught up in his mocking music that I'm not sure he even heard me.

They fell upon me then and the world became a confusing whirl of grit, muscle, motion, and the stink of the tobacco spittle that dripped from Peahead. Then came pain, the dull pain of repeated blows that pounded me like spikehammers and made me sink toward a floor that was beginning to spin beneath me. I tried to fight, but there can be no fighting when your main foe weighs twice what you do and doesn't mind using it to full advantage. How long this went on I did not know; time had come to a halt.

I heard my voice yelling for help, calling out to the fiddle player, the barkeep, anyone at all, to give me aid, but aid did not come. A fist struck my jaw and I called out no more. I felt tremendous weight atop me, felt the floor hard as an undertaker's slab beneath my back. My eyes, already swelling, opened enough to let me see the fearsome faces above, the massive fists that went up and down like shafts on a locomotive—and then a bare blade, glittering and sharp, that sliced open my shirt and exposed my chest. For some reason I noticed right then that the fiddle music had stopped.

I didn't hear Peahead speak, but he must have, because his partner said, "He says he's going to carve his initials on your chest for you to recollect him by."

I was near passing out when the knife pricked my chest. Writhing, I tried to pull free, but couldn't. The blade was cold and stinging. My eyes began to flutter shut and the images above me were almost gone when a third figure appeared behind the two that leaned over me. A heavy chair hovered, descended, crashed against the rocklike skull of Peahead. My last light dwindled and everything turned black. All I could hear as I sank away was the voice of the barkeep saying here now, don't do that, here now, don't do that, over and over.

The face that slowly put itself together before my blurry eyes was slender and brown and wore a mean expression. I groaned and swiped a hand across my eyes. When I looked again, the face was in sharper focus, and glittering somewhere below it was a badge on a blue shirt.

"What's your name?" the man with the badge demanded.

"McCan . . . Luke McCan," I answered in a whisper.

"Luke McCan, you think I need your ilk drifting through our town and stirring fights with the locals?"

"I . . . didn't stir any fight . . . just tried to help out . . ."

"You've helped yourself into a cell, that's what you've done. The barkeep says you lit into Peahead Jones with a spittoon, then fisticuffed with him and his brother before they raised a hand against you. Is that true?"

"The fiddler . . . they were slapping that fiddler . . ."

I pushed up a little and groaned. Somebody had put me on a bed in a small room. It might have been a spare bedroom in somebody's house, or maybe the sickroom of a doctor's office.

"It was to help out the fiddler that I got into it," I reaffirmed. I found a window to my right and looked out it. The sun was edging down.

"Well, this fiddler was gone when I got there, and the barkeep seems to hold you most at fault," the man with the badge said.

"He's a coward, then. Blaming it on me because he's afraid the other two will come back on him if he tells the truth."

"You can argue about it with the judge, Mr. McCan. You're under arrest on a charge of brawling, city ordinance number fifteen. However, if you'll make restitution for the saloon damages, I'll drop the charges and let you go. Fair enough?"

"Restitution? I'll pay no restitution for a fight I didn't start."

"Have it your way, then. If you won't do the responsible thing on your own, we'll let the city judge make the decision for you." The lawman reached over to a chest of drawers and fiddled with a pile of bills and change lying atop it. I recognized the prior contents of my pockets. "Let's see—three dollars and seven cents, a folding knife, and a handkerchief. Not a lot, but the cash I'll take to be applied toward your fine and the knife I'll take as a potential weapon. The handkerchief you can keep."

"Thanks very much. You're too kind." My attention was somewhat diverted from the lawman at the moment because I was examining my chest to see if there were any initials carved onto it. There weren't. The fiddler had brought that chair down on my attackers in time to save me a slicing.

"Old Doc says he wants you to stay here a few more hours so he can keep an eye on those bumps and bruises. I'm going to chain one of your ankles to the bed, in case you think you might like to run away. Tomorrow morning I'll move you to a cell, unless you've had more cooperative thoughts about paying that damage bill. Do you own a horse and saddle?"

"No." It wasn't really a lie, because the horse and saddle I possessed technically were property of my brother-in-law. In a way, you might say, I had stolen them from him, but not really, for he was dead when I took them. And he would have gladly given the horse and saddle to me, anyway, had he been alive. We got along well, my brother-in-law and I.

Without more talk the lawman produced a chain and linked me up firmly to the metal footboard. "That will do, and that's all for now. Good evening, Mr. McCan."

I gave an ill-tempered grunt in response, and closed my eyes. Every inch of me hurt, and from the feel of my face I knew I was probably no beautiful sight. But at least I was alive and uncut.

A little later a boy brought me supper on a tray. It must have been provided by the doctor, whom I had yet to talk to, rather than the jail, because this was better food than any jail would put up for a small-time prisoner like me. It was hard to chew the chicken because the left side of my jaw hurt every time I moved it. As I ate I wondered what had become of my pistol and gunbelt, which I had left hanging on the peg in the saloon. The lawman had not listed them among my personal effects, which must mean he was unaware of them. After supper I dozed off.

A pecking on the window beside the bed awakened me. I sat up. There was a face looking back in at me. It was lean, battered, familiar . . . the fiddler. He pecked lightly on the window again and made motions to indicate I should be careful and quiet.

The window was stuck, my muscles sore, and my ankle chained to the footboard; sliding up the lower window section proved difficult. With help of the fiddler outside I finally got the job done.

"Come on—I got your horse out here—we can ride out of this sorry town!"

"Not with me chained to a bed, I don't reckon."

He looked in over the sill, saw my situation, and swore beneath his breath. He clambered in through the window, making too much noise even though his thin, Lincolnesque form moved with the lightness of a wind-blown feather.

There proved to be strength as well as suppleness in those long limbs. He squatted at the end of the bed, wrapped a hand around the picketlike metal post I was chained to, and with a few grunts and twists worked it out of the footboard top-piece. My ankle chain slid off. The fiddle player stood and grinned.

"The name's J. W. Smith, but call me Fiddler," he said in a low voice. "You're . . ."

"McCan. Luke McCan."

"Pleased to know you, McCan, and thanks for your help today. This here's my way of repaying the favor."

"What's going on in there?" came a gruff voice from the other side of the door. The knob began to turn.

Fiddler Smith turned and dived headlong out the open window. Without a moment's hesitation I followed, hitting the ground with a grunt as the wind was knocked from me. I rose and ran, ankle chain jingling, struggling for breath that would not come, as behind me I heard the exclamation at discovery of empty room and open window. It gave me a joyful feeling, and as soon as breath returned, I laughed.

Chapter 2

We rode like wind blowing through a narrow mountain gap. For an hour we did not speak to each other, and we looked behind us often to see if there was sign of pursuit. There was none, and at last we slowed our pace to a lope, then a walk. Fiddler Smith's violin bounced on the side of his horse, hanging from the saddle horn in a large flour sack.

"Reckon I'm not enough of a criminal to merit a chase," I commented.

Fiddler Smith grinned. "Reckon not." He dug into his pocket and pulled out a twist of hot tobacco. Carving off a chew with his knife, he shoved the twist at me. I declined.

"Thanks for helping me out," I said.

"No, sir, it's me who owes thanks to you. Them two in that saloon might have done me in if you hadn't stepped in."

"You didn't look much scared, not with the way you kept on teasing that Peahead gent."

"I never had much sense, I admit. Once somebody pushes me, I push the other way. He gave me a hard time about my fiddling, so I gigged him about the lip." He grinned again. "Right mean of me. A man can improve his fiddling, but he can't change a harelip."

I reached down and touched the butt of my pistol, finding it reassuring to have it there again. "You must have took my gunbelt off the peg," I said. "I didn't figure I'd have it again."

"A man needs his weapons. Hey, that is your own horse I gave you, ain't it? It was the only one tied out front of the saloon. I figured it for yours."

"It's mine. Thanks for fetching it."

We rode a while longer, me sizing up Fiddler. He was an interesting-looking man and as ragged a one as I had ever seen. He wore nankeen trousers that had gone out of fashion a decade and a half back, a shirt that once had been yellow and now had faded to a sickly tan and white, and a dark broadcloth coat that hadn't been sponged down for a year or more. His hat was a battered derby greased from much handling. It fit his head as perfectly as a cartridge case around a slug.

We made camp in a grove beside a little stream. Fiddler gathered wood and built a roaring fire. I commented that maybe the fire was a bad idea, in that followers were still a possibility. Fiddler just shook his head.

"Never could abide to camp without a big fire," he said. "A man needs the comfort of light and heat out in the wilderness."

Fiddler had several cans of beans in his saddlebags and broke out two of them. I was glad to see them, being down to dried-up biscuits and a bag of jerky. My plan had been to resupply myself in town, a plan ruined by the row in the saloon.

After we had food under our belts, we fell to talking. Fiddler Smith spoke cheerfully—he seemed one of those types who are always cheerful—and told of a most unillustrious past.

"The mountains of West Virginia's where I come from—that'll always be home to me, though I doubt I'll ever again live in them. Never had a thing as a boy except two good parents. But they died young and left me alone, and that's how it's been for me ever since. My daddy left me nothing but that old fiddle yonder. My two sisters are dead these six and seven years, and the only brother I've got lives up in Powderville, Montana. I ain't seen him in twelve years.

"I took to roaming when I was sixteen. Even though I'm a slender fellow, I was a lot stouter in my younger days, and I've always been strong. The only two things I've ever known how to do is fight and fiddle, and that's how I've made my living. I'd fiddle in saloons, and toss out drunks who got too rowdy and such. Every now and again I'd serve as deputy or policeman in this or that town back east. Mostly I roamed through the cities, doing whatever I had to do to keep body and soul together. I was in Colorado awhile, too, at a little mining camp called Craig City. You might have heard of it."

"I think I have."

"McCan, I'll tell you, I ain't seen a bright prospect in a long time, not until now. Back when I was living in Chicago, I got myself fired from a saloon over a bit of trouble. Well, right after that into town comes this fellow named Walden, Ike Walden, a big white-haired man who called himself a 'freethinker for temperance and health.' He lived in a big house and had some sort of bee in his bonnet about closing down this saloon that had fired me—he claimed it was destroying the community or something like that.

"He held a big rally to close the place down and drew the biggest bunch of old women and teetotalers you ever saw. I was at the rally because of the food they were handing out. Things got hotter and wilder and before you know it, here goes Ike Walden and an army of these ax-carrying liquor-haters down to bust up the saloon. I went along, hoping to see the fellow who fired me get his come-uppance. Things got still hotter and before you know it, Ike Walden was staring down the barrel of a pistol. He decided to fight and was just about to get his brains blown out when I jumped up and wrestled my old boss to the ground and took the gun. To this day I ain't sure why I did it.

"Ike Walden declared me the finest fellow he had run across. He gave me a job doing general work around his place for almost a year. I got restless then and left for the West, but he told me to keep in touch with him and I did.

"Well, about two weeks ago I got a message from him, offering me new work. He's in Colorado now, and built himself a town about forty miles west of Fort Collins."

"What's the new work?"

Fiddler beamed with pride. "Town marshal. Town marshal of Walden City, Colorado mining town. Bound to be the best durn job I've run across."

"Can you handle it by yourself?"

Fiddler cocked his head and looked closely at

me. "Don't know. That's a good question. I'll tell you this—Walden's not allowing saloons or gambling in the town. He says that draws 'undesirable' folks. It seems to me that marshaling in a town without saloons and gambling halls ought to be a right easy job."

"Sounds like it."

Fiddler loaded and fired a corncob pipe. "Well, that's my story. Let's hear yours. You got family, McCan?"

There's no way Fiddler Smith could know the stab of pain that question brought to me. I doubt it showed on my face, for pain had been a constant companion of mine for months now, and I had grown accustomed to hiding it. I didn't want to answer his question, but given his openness with me, I felt obliged.

"I had family," I replied. "No wife, just a sister and her husband. And there would have been a wife by now, except . . ." My will failed me.

He gave a perceptive look. "She's dead?"

I nodded. "Not only her. My sister, too, and her husband. They were together on a train in Chatsworth, Illinois. It was last August when it happened. A railroad bridge caught fire and collapsed beneath the train. More than a hundred people died." I paused, my voice growing tight as it always did when I talked of this. "I was going to go with them at first, but at the last minute I had to stay behind. I was running a hardware store in Independence with my brother-in-law, you see, and our clerk quit on us just in time to knock me out of the trip. It saved my life, but when I think of what that accident took from me, I swear that sometimes I wish I had been on that train, too. Life without Cynthia hasn't been much of a life.''

"I'm sorry,'' Fiddler said.

"Me, too. Me, too.''

"So what brought you out here in the midst of this godforsaken territory?''

I rolled a smoke as I talked. "I wasn't brought out here. I was driven. Loneliness, mostly, and bad memories. After Cynthia, I didn't want to stay in Independence. The business didn't matter to me anymore, even though it passed to me after the . . . tragedy. I sold out, tucked some of the money into the bank to draw on as I needed, then took out roaming. Just like I did during my younger years. Roaming, working here and there. Mostly gambling. I gamble a lot. Too much. I had given it up for Cynthia, but after she was gone, it kind of reached out and took hold of me again.''

"You tell a sad story, McCan. Too sad to have happened to a fellow young as you. You can't be out of your twenties.''

"I'm well into the thirties now, Fiddler. I've always looked boyish, everybody tells me.''

"Losing a woman is hard for a man of any age. Look at it this way, McCan, there'll be other women. Odds are the next one you won't lose.'' .

"I've already lost two in my time.''

"Two?''

"Yes. Before Cynthia, there was a girl in Montana. Maggie Carrington was her name.''

"She died, too?''

"No, but as far as cutting herself off from me, she might as well have died. She married another man, name of Rodney Upchurch. Your talk about this Ike Walden and town-founding put me in mind of Upchurch. He set up the Upchurch community near Timber Creek."

"You talked about roaming in your younger days. Was that in Montana?"

"Mostly. I started out in Dakota. I freighted into Deadwood from Pierre during the big boom and stayed on to mine for a time with a man named Caleb Black."

"Caleb Black . . . sounds familiar." Fiddler drew on his pipe and his eyes suddenly lit up. "Wasn't it a Caleb Black who trailed the outlaw Evan Bridger for so many years?"

"One and the same."

"No! You mined with him? Well, I'll be, I'll be!"

"More than mined with him. We rode together up in Montana. I worked for the Timber Creek Cattle Enterprise, then finally just drifted out of the business and went back to Independence. That's tended to be my way, just drifting in and out of things, never settling down. Kind of funny, in a way. I thought when I met Cynthia that my wandering days were over. Now here I am, drifting again, shiftless as ever. I've already gambled away half of what I got from selling off the store."

"Montana," Fiddler said thoughtfully. "Sure got to get up to Montana myself one of these days, and see that brother of mine. Lord knows he might even be dead by now."

Fiddler sat quiet with his thoughts and eyed me through his pipesmoke for a while, then got up, stretched, and pulled his fiddle from its flour sack. He sat by the fire and played a couple of slow tunes, real strange and pretty, then laid down his bow and put the fiddle across his lap. I had gone to work on the ankle chain with a file from Fiddler's saddlebag. When at last the chain fell free, we both grinned. I rubbed my ankle in relief.

"Think you might want to cut out the drifting for a while and settle into some steady work?"

I shrugged. Fiddler must have found more yes than no in it, for he spread his easy grin again.

"In that case, why don't you stick with me and go to Walden City? Town marshaling might be too hard a job for one man, after all. I could use a deputy."

He surprised me with that one, I admit. "I don't know, Fiddler . . . this Ike Walden might not have in mind to hire more than you."

"Why, he feels he owes me. I can talk him into it or I ain't Fiddler Smith. What do you say, McCan? I like your company. You're good folks—I can spot it right off."

"Well . . . I got no other offers pending."

"That a yes?"

"Just a maybe. I can ride in with you and see how the place feels, and what this Ike Walden has to say."

Fiddler grinned all the broader. Picking up his fiddle again, he sawed out a new tune, this one lively and bright. I lit up my cigarette and lay back, smoking and watching the sky and wondering what kind of place Walden City would be, and whether I would stay there for any length of time.

A little later Fiddler brought out a bottle and took a long swallow. He waved the bottle at me but I turned it down.

"What's a champion of temperance like Ike Walden going to think of a town marshal who pulls on a flask on the side?" I asked him.

"Why, Ike Walden don't have to know everything," he replied. "And I don't have to be no angel of teetotalism to safeguard a town—at least as long as everybody else stays sober."

I chuckled, but the incident gave me my first pause as to the likelihood of Fiddler's success as a town marshal. Surely Ike Walden wouldn't put up with an enforcer who broke his own rules, not if he really was the authoritative type that Fiddler painted him.

We slept a little while and rode out with the dawn, crossing into Colorado just south of the South Platte. It would take some long traveling to reach Fort Collins, especially in that Fiddler planned to get there by way of Denver. Clearly he was in no real hurry to claim his new job, even though he seemed to be looking forward to it.

The longer we rode together, the better I got to know Fiddler Smith, and the greater my doubts about his ability to perform his awaited job became. He drank too much, usually not to the point of full drunkenness, but enough to become tipsy by sundown. "Don't worry," he reassured me. "I can hide it. Anyway, maybe a town without saloons will give me the nudge to throw the bottle away once and for all."

"Maybe so," I said. "And maybe a town without gambling halls will break me of my card habit."

Hours rolled into days and miles stretched behind us. We reached Denver and remained there three days, then rode north to Fort Collins and west into the rugged mountains, following the narrow trails that led to the new mining town of Walden City.

Chapter 3

Picture a trainload of new lumber hammered together into two rows of nondescript buildings, spread a wide street of mud between them, throw in abundant swinging shingles and windows with painted-on business signs, almost all incorporating the name "Walden," and you have a good image of what Walden City, Colorado, looked like the midmorning that Fiddler Smith and I finally rode in. There had been rain since dawn, and it had only just stopped, so the Walden City we saw was a wet one.

It was a typical new mountain town in most ways, built along the contours of the narrow valley in which it sat. The main street had a slight curve that was mandated by the rocky bluffs bumping up almost against the backsides of the row of buildings facing north. The opposite row wasn't so pressured and therefore in most mining camps would have been built straight, but here it curved right along with the other row, keeping the street a uniform width. I didn't understand the reason for that until I got to know Ike Walden. Then I knew: Walden wasn't the kind of man who would put up with irregular streets in any town bearing his name. Everything in Ike Walden's world was orderly, rigid, militarily precise. He permeated his town like the smell of fresh-cut pine lumber.

"She's a beaut, ain't she?" Fiddler Smith said as we slogged down the muddy street. He bent to the side and shot an amber dollop of tobacco juice into the mud. "This here town's going to be dancing to Fiddler and McCan's tune before long. We've come into our own, son, into our own."

Truth be told, though I was glad to be here, I wasn't nearly as excited as Fiddler. Maybe it was because I wasn't being awaited here, like he was, and so didn't feel the town was quite so much mine. Or maybe there was more to it. Maybe it was that beneath the town's facade of commonality with every other mining community, there was something remarkably different.

It took me a few minutes to realize what that was, and I chided myself for having been surprised by what I should have been expecting, considering Fiddler's earlier talk. The difference about Walden City was that among its plethora of buildings and businesses, there was not a single saloon. In most towns like this, a saloon was the first place built, before people got around to throwing up the less-important enterprises, such as hardware stores, restaurants, and livery stables. Niceties such as schools, churches, and doctors' offices usually came much later.

I scanned the buildings and picked out what looked like a brand-new schoolhouse still in the works. There was even a four-roomed hospital already open for business; a young medical-looking fellow stood leaning in its doorway, watching the bustle outside. I wondered if he would make much of a living in Walden City, given its lack of saloons and, presumably, knife-and gun-happy drunks.

"This Walden must be quite a powerful man, if he can dominate a whole town," I said to Fiddler.

"Dominate? Durn, he owns it!" Fiddler replied. "Most every one of these businesses here, he owns. Them he don't he leases out the buildings for. Even that there hospital belongs to him."

"How the devil did he manage to set up such a place?"

"Friends in high places, as the phrase goes. He worked out some special grant of land up here, some deal there ain't nobody else got. He even controls all the mineral rights—gold, silver, everything. I don't understand it all that much, but suffice it to say, this here town is Ike Walden's all the way, and anything you get you get only because he deals it out to you. There may not be kings and such in this country of ours, but there sure as Sally is a king in Walden City."

We turned down what would eventually become a side street but which was now only a short, rutted thoroughfare with a handful of small houses and huts along it. Our horses splashed through a deep puddle of brown water, beyond which the fledgling street became a lane, then a mere trail that threaded into the trees.

"Where we going?" I asked.

"Open your eyes, McCan! Were you so smit with that muddy town that you didn't look up on the hillside?"

I looked now; through a gap in the trees I saw a house, painted a neat white, perched on a plateau above the western end of the town. From its front window you could look right down the center of the street. It wasn't all that big a house—just a typical two-story that would have looked modest in an Eastern city neighborhood—but it had a pretentious round tower and was set high up enough that it seemed bigger than it was. As I studied it, a shaft of sunlight cut through the clouds and gleamed off the white clapboards, making the house stand out against the mountains like a diamond among pebbles.

"That's got to be Walden's house," I said.

"Reckon so. His letter described the place right well. 'The Walden Palace,' he calls it."

"Palace, huh? Well, it's got a tower, but it falls pretty far short of a palace."

"Don't get picky about Ike Walden or his things. He's not a man who likes pickiness in other folk. He figures that being picky is his job."

We circled up the trail and onto the big flat on which the house stood. We approached it from the side. Glancing up the tower, I saw a figure standing in the big window row that curved all the way around the top. I couldn't make out much about him other than that he was portly but tall and had a gray topknot and long hair that stuck out wide on both sides of his head. It made him look from here like some wild-eyed Puritan expositor from long ago.

Fiddler threw up his arm and waved eagerly at the figure, smiling brightly. The man in the tower stood up straight and waved back, very dignified and haughty. So far my impressions of Ike Walden were falling out just as I expected they would.

We dismounted beside the house and were about to tether our horses to a tree when out of the house

came two black servants, both wearing uniforms
that made them look like railroad-station baggage
carriers. "We'll be happy to take your horses, gentlemen sirs," one of them said. "If one of you
gentlemen sirs is Mr. J. W. Smith, Mr. Walden is
waiting to see you."

"I'm Smith," Fiddler said. "This here's my
partner, Luke McCan. You want we should just
walk in?"

"I'll show you in, Mr. Smith, sir," the servant
said. He had a beaten-down look in his eye, and
you could tell at once that being handservant to the
king of Walden City was a draining job. I felt sorry
for him.

He led us into the house, which was as spanking
new as the rest of the town but more finished. I
figured Walden had seen to the completion of his
"palace" before anything else. The interior was
fancy, though again only in comparison to the rest
of the town. In any other setting it would have been
nice but nothing to gape at. There was carpet and
wainscoting and a shiny ceiling, but a close look
revealed seams and gaps that showed the place was
rather hastily built.

The servant took us over to a big oak door that
was still awaiting a sanding down and a coat of
paint. It creaked open to reveal a circular staircase,
made of rough lumber, leading to the tower.

"You sirs will need to take care 'cause there
ain't yet no banister," the servant said. He began
plodding up the stairs. We followed, making one
full circle around the tower before we reached the
landing at the top and faced another oak door.

The servant knocked, then opened a little metal
slide three quarters of the way up the door and

through it said, "Mr. Walden, sir, Mr. J. W. Smith and his partner Mr. McCan are come to see you."

"Bring them in, then, Bob," came a booming voice. I was thinking how peculiarly formalized this process was, given that Walden had already seen us through his window and we had seen him. I suppose a "king" has to maintain some sort of protocol when he gives audience to his subjects.

As the door swung open, I was already thinking to myself that I wasn't going to like Ike Walden much, not if such airs as this were common to him. Ever since I had had trouble with a pompous little Iowa-born snoot named Henry Sandy back at the Timber Creek ranch in Montana, arrogance had set poorly with me.

Walden was a broadcloth expanse of belly, vest, and watch fob, peaked off with a wide and somewhat pasty face. What I had from a distance taken for long hair hanging down either side of his head actually were big stiff sideburns that ran down almost to his deeply dimpled chin. He had no mustache, but needed one: the space between his mouth and the bottom of his little nose seemed overly wide and could have used some filling in.

"J. W., it's good to see you," he said to Fiddler, thrusting out his delicate hand. "I can't tell you how thrilled I am that you've accepted the job."

"I've been slow to get here, Mr. Walden," Fiddler said. "I hope that ain't given you no problems."

"None at all, sir. We have peaceful folk in this town." He glanced at me. "Mr. McCan—isn't that the name you gave?"

"Luke McCan. Pleased to meet you, Mr. Walden." His handshake was soft and moist, the kind that leaves you conscious of your own palm and makes you want to wipe it on your pants leg, which of course you can't do.

"I'm glad to know you, sir, but I admit to being at a loss. I had expected only Mr. Smith."

Fiddler stepped forward. "Mr. Walden, McCan here is a longtime partner of mine. We've known each other for years, and he's a fine man with peace-officer experience. He and me served together under Masterson back in my early days at Dodge City."

I fired a shocked glance at Fiddler, who was lying through his tobacco-coated teeth. He had laid out his life fairly thoroughly to me by now, and had never mentioned being a deputy in Dodge—and I sure as heck knew I had never been. Obviously Fiddler had greatly inflated his credentials to Walden even before now, for the Dodge City reference had been given in the easy manner of a mutually familiar subject.

"Well, I'm impressed, then," Walden said. "Am I to presume you wish Mr. McCan to assist you in the job?"

"Well, sir, I had hoped you'd consider it."

Walden scratched the deep cleft in his chin and looked at me in a way to make me feel like I was on an auction block. His brows came down in an evaluative frown, then he shook his head.

"I have nothing in the budget for an assistant, even one who looks as fit and promising as this young man," he said, making me feel flattered even in rejection.

"Oh, he'll work for free," Fiddler promptly replied. "All he requires is room and board."

I didn't even try to hide my glare of shock, but

Walden had gone into a coughing fit and was looking down, hacking into his fist, and didn't see it.

When he had cleared his throat, he begged our pardon and picked up where Fiddler had left off, "Labor in return for only room and board? Are you really willing to do that, Mr. McCan?"

"Well, actually I—"

"McCan is a former hardware-store man out of Independence, Missouri," Fiddler chirpily interrupted. "He sold out his business and is fairly well off, and might set up in trade right here, if he likes the place." I could only listen in amazement as Fiddler revealed to Walden plans and dreams even I didn't know I had. "Free room and board in return for some part-time marshaling would set him ahead just enough to make this town a mighty appealing place for him—and I could surely use his help from time to time."

Walden seemed impressed. I started to speak up to burst the bubble of illusion Fiddler was blowing—then I decided abruptly not to. Making Fiddler out for the liar he was might cost him the job he had come for, and I didn't want that to happen. Besides, it would be fun to see what Walden would say.

"Well . . . well . . . all right, then. There's a small house set aside for you behind the jail, Mr. Smith. With only a little effort and expense I can quickly add another room . . . if Mr. McCan is serious in this offer."

I opened my mouth, honestly not knowing what I was going to say. What came out was, "I'm serious." What the devil, I was thinking. I've got nowhere else to go, I've got to stay somewhere, and a free room is better than one with a price tag.

"Fine, then, fine," Walden said. Suddenly he faced me and spoke in a surprisingly forceful tone. "You understand, I hope, that in Walden City I tolerate no drunkards or opium fiends, no gamblers, sluggards, harlots, or any such ilk?"

"I understand. Fiddler . . . Mr. Smith, I mean, has told me all about it."

"Good. And no preachers, either. Purveyors of unscientific superstition have no place in Walden City. We are overshadowed not by steeples but by reason, by intelligence and rationality. If anyone waves a Bible on a street corner in this town, you may summarily escort them past our borders, gentlemen."

"Seems to me a good preacher or two might help you keep out the gamblers and drunkards you despise so."

Walden's eyes seemed to pop in their sockets. He stepped forward, suddenly a foot taller than before. "I am a freethinker, Mr. McCan, unfettered by belief in some bearded overseer on a heavenly throne. This is my town. It will operate in accordance with my lights, not yours. If you work for me, you must understand that."

I said nothing. He stared at me a moment or two, then his harshness faded and he smiled. "You understand me, I can see. I like you, McCan. You have a healthful look about you—the kind of man who can serve as a good example for the people of this town." He looked at Fiddler. "And I must confess, Mr. Smith, that I detect in your eyes the tracks left by the beast alcohol. I do hope you'll not fail to live up to the standards I require."

"No fear of that, Mr. Walden. I know what you expect."

"Good. Very good. Now, if you gentlemen will return downstairs, I'll join you in a moment and show you your new office and quarters."

While we were waiting below, I commented, "Strange character."

"No doubt of that. But once you get used to him he ain't bad."

"I'm talking about you, not him. What was all that Dodge City nonsense, and when did I tell you I was willing to work just for lodging?"

"Well, you took the bargain, didn't you? Shows I was right."

A door across the room opened and in walked a woman who was obviously barely into her twenties. She was rather plump but very pretty, even though her eyes were red as if she had been recently crying. She stopped short when she saw us, stared at me for a couple of moments, then withdrew quickly back into the door from which she had come.

"Who was that?" I asked.

"Vera Ann Walden, Ike's daughter. He's a widower, you see. Pretty thing, ain't she!"

"Easy enough on the eyes, I suppose." I felt prideful over the way she had looked at me. "Did you notice how she—"

"How she looked at me?" Fiddler cut in. "You bet I did. Reckon I must be a handsomer gent than I had thought."

I stood with my mouth half-open, on the verge of correcting his obvious misperception. No—it wasn't worth it. "You are a fine-looking specimen of a man, now that I notice it," I said.

"Wish I could say the same for you."

"You can. All you got to do is lie about it like

I did. Ought to be no difficulty for you. I've had occasion to notice today that you're adept with the falsehoods.''

He just grinned. That was a good thing about Fiddler Smith: You could gig him and he'd take it without a flinch . . . most of the time.

Chapter 4

We had thought it would be an easy job. No saloons, no faro halls, no houses of prostitution—yet the people of Walden City proved to be the most ill-tempered, fight-mongering, downright sorry gaggle I had ever had the misfortune to run across. I commented to Fiddler that Walden City was like Deadwood in its early days, minus the vice. That's the very problem, Fiddler responded. Folks here don't have any way to let the steam off their boilers.

It took me less than a week to realize that Ike Walden's grand experiment in "rational temperance," as he called his civic philosophy, was doomed to fail. A lot of the people of Walden City were devoted followers of Walden and had migrated here with him, determined to make his dream a reality. But as many were followers in name only, their chief lure being the silver mines. Sure, they signed their names on Walden's line, as required to stake a claim in his territory. They agreed to use no liquor or opium, to follow his list of rules to the letter, and to make no attempts to form any religious or political bodies. Even so, be-

fore our first three weeks were behind us, Fiddler
and I had busted up three illegal stills, run a wagon-
load of prostitutes out of town, broken up an on-
going faro operation, and given warning to two
street-corner preachers. The last duty I had left to
Fiddler alone; even though those times long pre-
ceded my church-going days, I didn't think it right
to interfere with folks' religion. And from a strictly
practical viewpoint, such bullying never worked,
anyway. You can turn a people against you by denying them their righteousness just as quick as by
denying them their sin, and Walden was doing
both.

I made such observations to Fiddler late one evening after a particularly hard day. He responded by
picking up his fiddle and scratching out an accom-
paniment as he sang a funny old cowboy tune about
a freethinker in a cattle camp whose mouthing
against religion earned him an opinion-changing
whipping from a big brawling cowpoke who declared he wouldn't hear his mother's religion dis-
paraged. As I pen this narrative all these years later,
I can still hear Fiddler's coarse but pleasant voice
stringing out that last line: ". . . and the spread of
infideliteeeeee . . . was checked in camp that day."
Then came the fiddle's final flourish, done in a
characteristic and indescribable style I had never
heard any other string-sawer employ.

Fiddler Smith, I had already learned, gave his
thoughts in his music as much as in his spoken
word. In the brief time I had known him, I had
come to like the man a lot. He was an entertaining,
easygoing companion with whom I could be at
ease.

But he had another side, one that didn't put me

at ease at all. Just as I had feared, he did not put aside his drinking after coming to the "town of scientific temperance." Where he got his bottles I never knew, but he always had one. Walden City had some underground liquor market that didn't run dry. It was more evidence that "King Ike" Walden, as some snickeringly called him, didn't exercise the deep control he thought he did.

King Ike, nonetheless, was for the time being firmly ensconced as the fountainhead of law in Walden City. He served as city judge and head of the town board, comprised entirely of his staunchest followers. Fiddler and I sat in on one of its meetings two days after our arrival; we were there primarily to be introduced. It was the most peculiar meeting I had ever attended. Little real town business was discussed. Mostly the event consisted of Ike Walden talking about his views, which he wrapped up in scholarly sounding jargon and dubbed the "new scientific gospel of human welfare." I didn't understand much of it, maybe because of my lack of education at that time, or maybe because there really wasn't much there to understand in the first place.

Walden's court, like his town board meetings, was equally a platform for his expositions. The courthouse, on the outside a plain plank building, was much fancier inside. It was almost churchlike, with pews lined up facing a raised stage on which a big desk sat beside a humble witness box. On the desk was Walden's motto: "Science, Temperance, and Freedom from Superstition." I witnessed many of the "trials" he conducted with his selected jury, and though I knew little of law, it was clear even to me that there was nothing legal about these farcical hearings. Walden's "criminals" ranged from merchants who failed to pay sufficient city sales taxes to drunks and gamblers. All were found guilty; all were evicted from the town by the pompous self-declared judge.

"This can't last," I told Fiddler after one of these sessions. "A real lawyer could take Walden to a real court and burst his bubble with one prod."

"You'll notice," Fiddler replied, "that there ain't no real lawyers in this town."

He was right, and that was another peculiarity of Walden City. Most mining towns swarmed with attorneys, both good and bad, but there were only two law offices in Walden City, both occupied by Walden-appointed men. For all I knew, neither one had any valid legal training.

It didn't take me long to decide that my days in Walden City were to be short. Not long could I continue to play a part in Walden's ridiculous drama and live with my conscience. At the end of the first month I told Fiddler I was thinking of leaving and urged him to do the same. He seemed dismayed, and begged me to reconsider.

"Why?" I asked. "Walden's bound to be brought down before a year goes by. I figure we can get out with our pride, or get tossed out looking as foolish as he is."

"Hell, you don't know he's going to go down, McCan," Fiddler replied. "This here's a remote town; ain't nobody much on the outside who even knows how it runs."

"Let Walden keep running people off and pretty soon the word will spread," I replied.

"Well, when that happens it'll be time to go. As it is, we got us a good situation until then. This is the first good-paying job I've ever had, McCan, but I can't do it without help. Dang, you've got a free place to stay and run of the whole city—why not stay on while it lasts?''

It had always been one of my flaws that I was too easily talked into things that my common sense told me were mistakes. Fiddler's hangdog plea hit me in a soft spot. Sighing, I said, ''All right. I'll stay for now, though I can't see what you find so all-fired great about scraping for King Ike.''

Fiddler grinned. ''It ain't the king that holds me—it's the princess.'' With that he turned away, went into his room, and closed the door. In a moment fiddle music came wafting through, broken by short pauses that I knew marked pulls from another hidden bottle.

The princess . . . he had to mean Vera Ann Walden. It was the first hint I had received that he had been seeing Walden's plumpish daughter on the sneak. Before long the hints would grow stronger.

Fiddler Smith and Vera Ann Walden. The combination smelled of trouble from the beginning, for by now I had seen enough to know that King Ike's heavy hand lay heaviest on his own single child. He guarded her like a treasure, and I doubted any man who tried to take that treasure away would be spared Walden's wrath.

I should have gotten out then. Should have, but didn't.

The next day Ike Walden called me up to his house. This is it, I figured. He's heard something bad on me and I'm about to be gone . . . which might be the best thing to happen, come to think of it.

But Walden surprised me. He called me into his

tower sanctum, handed me a long cigar, and told me he had authorized a salary for me almost equal to Fiddler Smith's. I was so surprised I dropped the cigar and scorched his rug. Walden didn't even seem to mind.

"I like you, McCan," he said. "You inspire confidence in a way that—I must speak frankly— your superior doesn't. You're fit, strong, young, reliable. Marshal Smith, on the other hand, seems to have lived an unhealthy life. I suspect he doesn't hold to the principles on which this town is built. Tell me, have you any knowledge as to whether Marshal Smith might be drinking liquor in secret?"

My surprise over being given a salary faded into a suspicion that I was being plied. Walden wanted to use me as a source of damning information about Fiddler. I wondered if Fiddler's drinking was the only reason Walden was turning against the man he had specifically sought out for the marshal's post.

"If you don't mind me saying, Mr. Walden, if you have personal questions about Marshal Smith, maybe you ought to put them to him, not me."

Walden's expression soured and for half a second it looked like he might get mad. Whatever he was about to say he swallowed down, though, and drummed his fingers on his desk as he said, "Perhaps you're right, Mr. McCan. My reason for coming to you first is that I would hate to confront Marshal Smith on so important a matter if I've misinterpreted his situation. He'd have justification for being angry about that."

"I suppose he would, but I think he'd be more likely to be angry if he found out you'd been asking behind his back. That's my opinion, at least."

Walden nodded briskly, his lips tightly shut. It crossed my mind that it was a good thing he'd already promised me the salary, for now that I wasn't cooperating with him like he wanted, he didn't seem quite as happy with me.

And maybe he wasn't, but he still had another surprise for me anyway. He obviously saw it as a positive one. My own feelings were different.

"There's a special favor I'd like to ask of you, Mr. McCan," he said. "My daughter, Vera, wants to go into town to buy a couple of dresses. I'd like you to accompany her."

"Beg pardon?"

"I said I'd like you to accompany her. Look out for her, you know."

I was confused. "Is Miss Walden in some sort of danger?"

"No, no, not specifically . . . well, not danger as such." He licked his lips and looked uncomfortable. "Mr. McCan, let me tell you something in confidence. My daughter has fallen victim to some sorry rumors—damnable things, slurs against her character. I won't dignify them by repetition. Let me assure you, they are unjustified. My Vera Ann is a staunch, upright, dignified young woman. I've raised her free of superstition but have given her a strong moral base. Yet there are those who like to spread lies. I'll ferret them out and rid this town of them soon enough, let me assure you.

"But in the meantime, I hate for her to be on the streets alone, where she might be humiliated by some loose-tongued scoundrel. I want her with someone I can trust. That's you, McCan." He cleared his throat. "I can trust you, can't I?"

Indeed he could, where Vera Ann was concerned. She was as appealing to me as a feeder pig in skirts. Vera Ann was the Lord's positive answer to the prayer "Lead us not into temptation." It was Fiddler Smith's chime she rang, not mine.

And that was one reason I didn't want to have to become her escort. I wanted nothing to do with the lady whose secret relationship with Fiddler Smith was bound to get back to her father's ears. Nor did I relish the thought of walking around Walden City with a lady folks were whispering about.

None of it made a difference. There was no way to turn down Walden's request, not after he had just handed me a big salary and a potful of praise. "I'll do whatever I can to see to her safety, Mr. Walden," I glumly replied.

He smiled now. "Thank you, Mr. McCan. I don't forget those who display a willing and helpful attitude—you'll see that."

He reached over to his desk and picked up a bell. Its jingle brought Bob, the servant, to the office door.

"Tell Vera Ann that Mr. McCan will be waiting for her below," he said. "Tell her not to make him have to dawdle around overlong."

"No hurry," I said. "I'll just finish smoking this cigar while I wait."

The cigar was long gone by the time Vera Ann finally came down the stairs. She smiled brightly at me with that pretty-but-plump face, and I found myself seeing things in that smile that I might just be imagining but probably wasn't. I dreaded this. Before nightfall half of Walden City would have seen me walking around with King Ike's ill-reputed daughter and I'd probably never hear the end of it.

"Thank you so much for escorting me, Mr.

McCan,'' she said, slipping her arm under mine. She smelled strongly of perfume and powder. ''Daddy worries a lot for me ever since my . . . trouble began.''

''I'll try to make sure you're in good hands,'' I said as we went out the door. At once I realized what a poor choice of words that was.

But Vera Ann apparently did not. She leaned over to me and whispered into my ear: ''I wouldn't mind that, I don't think.''

I couldn't find a single thing to say. I pretended to go into a sneezing fit so I could pull myself free of her as I dug my rag of a bandanna out of my pocket. The ploy only worked for a moment, for her arm slid right back into place. Together we walked down the curving path that led down from Ike Walden's ''palace'' to the town, me feeling Walden's gaze on us from his big tower window all the way.

Chapter 5

Vera Ann's expression combined sympathy and admiration as she dabbed at my bleeding lip with a lacy handkerchief pulled from her purse.

"Oh, you poor thing," she said, standing too close as she tended me. "Bless your heart, you've hurt yourself fighting over me."

"It's not that much," I said. "Just a split lip—you needn't do any more, thanks." I pulled away.

Her face was tear-streaked and red. "Oh, Luke—can I call you Luke?—you don't know what it means to me that you defended me against that, that . . . insulting scoundrel."

The time was exactly one hour after I left Walden's house with Vera Ann hanging on my arm. And a more uncomfortable hour I couldn't recall. Vera Ann had walked beside me like she was pasted to my hip, keeping such perfect beat with my stride that we must have looked like a two-headed, two-gendered monster stumping down the boardwalk. It felt like every eye in Walden City was on us; many were the grins and nudges I noted in the corner of my eye as I stared straight ahead.

Vera Ann had steered me into a dress shop,

where she poked around among the most expensive frocks and made agonizingly slow selections. I muttered something about going out onto the porch for a smoke and escaped after about ten minutes.

A glitter-eyed fellow with an aggravating grin slid up beside me. "What's your boss man going to think about you running 'round with Vera Ann, huh?" he asked smirkingly.

I figured at first that he was talking about Ike Walden and replied that it was my "boss man" himself who had sent me out with her. His eyes widened.

"Fiddler Smith sent you out with his own woman?" he asked disbelievingly.

"Not Fiddler—Ike Walden."

"Oh! Fiddler won't like that much, I bet." He grinned again and started to go away.

"Wait a minute—just what do you know about Fiddler and Vera Ann?"

"Same thing everybody else in the dang town knows. Them two have been sparking like two hot coals right under King Ike's nose." He winked. "Old King Ike don't look kindly on it, either, from what I hear."

The man walked away, leaving me feeling uncomfortable and unhappy. Fiddler's relationship with Vera Ann was between him and her, and, I supposed, between them and Ike Walden. I didn't like being thrown into the mix just because Ike didn't like his daughter keeping company with my immediate superior.

Three cigarettes later, Vera Ann came out with her new dresses wrapped in brown paper parcels. Though I didn't feel particularly gentlemanly at the moment, I took them from her. "I'll carry these back up to the house for you."

She took my arm and squeezed it. "Oh, let's not go back yet," she said. "I'd sure like to have a piece of pie and some coffee first."

I was tempted to sigh in displeasure but politely held it in. "All right. Lead on."

She led me across one of the wide walkways laid across the muddy street, and toward a little cafe. That was where it happened.

A big bearded miner stepped forward. "Howdy, there, Vera Ann," he said, grinning at her and acting as if I wasn't even there. "How about you and me having a little fun this evening?"

Vera Ann pulled back and closer to me. She looked offended and scared. I stepped between her and the man.

"I don't like your tone, friend," I said.

"I don't recall talking to you, curly," he replied coldly.

"My name's McCan. I'm the assistant marshal here, and I suggest you go on about your business elsewhere."

He was twice as big as me and looked tough enough to eat horseshoes for breakfast. "I don't care if you're the president's first cousin," he said. "My business is with Vera Ann." He leered in a way that raised my hackles. "And I hear tell she likes the kind of business I got in mind."

The rest you can easily picture for yourself. By the time our row was finished, the big fellow was too busy tending his broken nose to care about "business" anymore, and I was striding with Vera Ann back across the street, my split lip putting the taste of blood on my tongue. I could have arrested the man, but I felt too disgusted and mad to bother with it.

For half the distance back to Walden's home I didn't say a word to Vera Ann. People stared at us all the way. At last she managed to squelch her tears, pulled out her handkerchief, and began tending to my lip and talking to me as described before.

"Vera Ann," I said, "do you want me to tell your father what happened?"

She looked at me with horror. "No! Please don't! He wouldn't . . . understand."

I had my doubts about that. Probably he would understand, maybe already did. His daughter obviously had the reputation in Walden City of being a loose woman.

"All right," I said. "I'll say nothing. But let me tell you this, you obviously need to be careful about the way you . . ."

Her tears threatened to come again. "About what? What are you trying to say?"

"Nothing. Never mind. Let's just get you home."

This time Ike wasn't in his big window, to my relief. At the door Vera Ann surprised me with a hug. "You're a wonderful man, Luke McCan," she said. "I feel safe when I'm with you. I like that."

I mumbled something vague.

"Maybe we can do this again," she said, seemingly having forgotten already what a humiliating experience this had been for both of us. "Please come back . . . I like you a lot." Suddenly she became intense. "This town is no place for you, any more than it is for me. Let's leave. Together."

"What?"

"I've got to get away from here, away from Father. Soon."

"You're talking to the wrong man, Vera Ann."

"No, I'm not. You're the rightest man I ever met." She hugged me again. "Think about it—but don't think too long."

Never before was I as glad to get away from a place and a person as I was when I plodded back down the hill to town. My lip was starting to throb and swell now, and I headed home to see how bad the damage was.

It was nothing serious, just a little cut from my own tooth. I slapped some of Fiddler's whiskey on it to clean it, then lay down on my bunk to calm down. I wound up falling asleep.

When I woke up, Fiddler was there, slumped in his chair at the table, looking at me sternly.

"Who lit into you?" he asked.

"Does the lip look that bad?"

"Puffed up like a riled cat."

"It's nothing. I had a little go-around with a rude fellow on the street."

Fiddler was filling a pipe. "Yeah. I heard about it. Everybody in town's talking about it."

"Wouldn't you know it."

He fired the tobacco. "What were you doing out with Vera Ann?"

"Ike put me to it. He asked me to go with her to buy some dresses. Apparently he's got the idea that people in this town have funny ideas about his little girl." I touched my sore lip. "It seems he's right."

Fiddler sat up straight. "What's that supposed to mean?"

"I doubt I need to explain it."

He puffed the pipe vigorously, and fumed more than it did. "I don't like you catting around with Vera Ann."

"It wasn't my choice. Like I said, Ike Walden put me to it. I was just doing my job." I paused, wondering whether to go on. "He's picked up some rumors about you and her, Fiddler."

He said nothing, just sat smoking until the pipe went out. "I'm hungry," he said. "Think I'll open us a can of beans."

For the rest of the evening, we had little to say to each other.

I found them together the next evening when I came home unexpectedly to fetch a new sack of tobacco. Fiddler was in his long johns and Vera Ann in her petticoat. She screeched and hid on the other side of Fiddler's bed when I came through the door.

"McCan, what the devil are you doing here?" Fiddler bellowed.

"I might ask you the same—except I can figure out the answer for myself."

"A man can't have no privacy, it appears," he said angrily.

"It's my place, too. If I had known, I'd have stayed away."

Vera Ann began to cry. "Don't tell my father, please!"

"Don't fret. I'm a man who minds my own business."

"You could at least have the decency to turn your head," Fiddler growled.

I did turn away, digging into my trunk for the tobacco. When I turned again Vera Ann had her dress back on and Fiddler was in his trousers.

"I'm leaving," I said. "And I'll knock the next time I come in." I glanced at Vera Ann and noticed her face was very white. "Are you all right?"

Her answer was to stumble back to the other side of the bed again and get sick on the floor. Fiddler made a face, then looked worried.

"Honey, I didn't know you were sick! What's wrong?"

"Nothing," she said weakly, straightening. "I want to go home."

"I'll take you," Fiddler said.

"No, no, Father's there. He'll see you."

"Well, I can't let you go alone, not with you sick."

"I'm not sick. Really I'm not." She turned a pleading face to me. Her color was starting to return. "Luke can take me."

Fiddler didn't appear to like that idea any more than I did. Under the circumstances, though, he could say nothing.

Along the way she hugged close to me like before. "Have you thought about it?" she asked.

"Listen, Vera Ann," I said. "I can't take you away from here. It just wouldn't be the thing to do."

She pulled away. "Why? Do you believe all the bad things people say about me?"

"What I believe doesn't matter. It just wouldn't work. I'm not looking for female company right now. I was going to be married not long ago, and I lost her. She died. It'll be a long time before I can get past that."

She looked at me in silence. "Then I'll just have to get Fiddler to take me away."

"Why do you want to go so bad? You've got a good life here, a good home . . ."

"There's nothing good here, and it's going to get worse. A lot worse." She looked like she might cry again. This was the most emotional young woman I had ever met, so much so that I began to wonder if there was something wrong with her, if maybe she really was sick.

And then it came to me. I understood.

"Why are you staring at me like that?" she asked.

"Never mind," I said. "Come on, let's get you home."

I left her at the door, happy that there was no light up in Walden's tower office. I had escaped being seen by him.

Fiddler was drunk and playing his fiddle when I got back later that night. Once again I had been left to patrol Walden City on my own.

"You been funning around town with my woman again?" he asked.

"Nope. I've been out doing my job—our job, if you'd take more part in it."

"I reckon I do what I should. How I handle my job is between me and Ike Walden."

"That's not all that's going to be between you, once he figures out the truth."

"Truth about what?"

"About Vera Ann. It looks pretty clear to me. Her getting sick, her all fired up to get out of Walden City as soon as she can . . ."

"How do you know about that?"

"She talks about it. That girl has got something to hide from her father that she won't be able to hide much longer."

"Talk straight, man!"

"Can't you see it, Fiddler? Vera Ann's pregnant."

He didn't say a thing, but slowly went as white as Vera Ann had been earlier. He spun around in his chair, turning his back to me, picked up his bottle, and took a long, bubbling swallow.

Chapter 6

If Ike Walden had thought his influence was broad enough to keep vice away from his part of the world, he quickly learned otherwise. Shortly after I found Vera Ann and Fiddler together, a saloon began going about a mile east of town. In what had been an empty mountain meadow a pile of lumber appeared one day, and by the next afternoon most of the shell of a large building stood there, with word spreading that this was to be a full-fledged saloon.

King Ike was infuriated to see this moral incursion at the border of his kingdom. Fiddler came in grinning the night after the board siding went up on the building, saying Ike and he had ridden out to the site so Ike could voice his formal protest. The answer had been a sawed-off shotgun fired into the sky by one of the handful of men working on the building. King Ike had hauled his royal self back to Walden City as fast as his horse could carry him, Fiddler chortled.

Out on the streets, the new saloon was the talk of everyone. Lots of people began riding out to the site, watching the building go up and wondering when the liquor would be freighted in. A few of Walden's sincere followers seemed distressed by this development. Most others were openly delighted. Clearly, Ike Walden's hatred of demon rum was not going to staunch its flow outside his jurisdiction, nor would he be able to halt the flow of his people from town to tavern.

Walden called Fiddler and me into his tower office for a conference about the saloon. As he paced the floor, smoking one of his big cigars and shaking ashes all over the place, he raged and declared that any Walden Citian who came into the city drunk from the saloon would face the most severe punishment, either jail time or banishment, whichever they chose.

"You're likely to deplete your population, then," Fiddler declared. "You can't ride herd on everything folks want to do."

Walden turned a fierce gaze on his marshal. "That's a particularly interesting comment, coming from you," he said. He didn't explain what he was getting at. He didn't need to.

I confess that I was among those who were glad to see the saloon going up. My Walden City days were one of several low times I've had in my life, the loss of my beloved one being still fresh. The call of the long-missed gambling table was strong. With my own eyes I witnessed a roulette wheel and faro table being unloaded at the saloon; the effect on me was like that of a finely roasted steak laid out before a starving man. The gambling fever took hold and I knew that at first chance I would be in that saloon, scratching the familiar old itch.

The day I saw the gambling equipment unloaded was the day I first saw the big Indian. When I say big, I mean big. He towered over every other man there by a good six inches, was as broad as a wagon, and sleekly muscled like a puma. Beyond that there was nothing sleek about him; he was grizzled and harsh and ragged-edged. Across the middle of his face ran a harsh scar that mangled his nose to gristle—and most remarkable of all, he had a missing ear. Just like Fiddler.

I watched him from a distance, and saw from his manner and motions that he was a man of some authority. He himself worked hard, hefting around big stacks of planks as if they weighed nothing, but also directed other laborers.

"See the redskin?" came a voice from behind me. I turned in my saddle and saw a blond-haired miner riding up beside me. "That's one of the proprietors of this fine new establishment."

"That right?"

"Yes sir. His name's Jim. Big Jim the Scarnose. He's a Sioux, or at least mostly Sioux. Likely he's been a bit mongrelized along the way."

I stuck out my hand. "McCan's the name."

We shook. "I'm Baker. Tate Baker. Don't even think about calling me Tater."

"I wouldn't. How do you know so much about the saloon yonder?"

"Why, I just rode up yesterday and asked. I'm looking forward to seeing it opened, I don't mind telling you."

"You don't sound like one of Ike Walden's devoted."

"I ain't. Walden's crazy, in my book." Tate Baker suddenly gave me a shocked look. "Say, ain't you the marshal?"

"Assistant marshal."

He cast up his eyes. "Lord, Tate, you've gone and done it now!" he said. Then to me: "Look, please forget what I said. Don't go tattling back to Walden about me coming out here. I don't want to lose my claim."

"Don't worry. I work for Walden, but I'll be danged if I'm going to be his eyes and ears."

Tate grinned slyly. "Walden City's assistant marshal ain't too happy in his job, I take it?"

"You take it right. And as far as I'm concerned, you can take the job, too. I don't aim to hold it much longer."

"I don't blame you. It's rough just living in Walden's town. It's got to be even rougher working for him."

"It's got its pressures, let's put it that way. And there's a hot situation that's likely to explode soon." I looked wistfully across the clearing. "Still, it seems an odd time to think of leaving, now that a saloon is coming in. I like to gamble."

Tate chuckled. "What do you know! Ike Walden's lawman's going to sneak off on the side to flirt with vice!"

The comment made me think about Fiddler and Vera Ann—the explosive situation I had subtly mentioned. Walden's control of his "kingdom" was breaking down, just as I had expected. It wouldn't be pleasant to work under him as it all crumbled. The time to get out was now.

But as I left Baker and rode back to town, I was thinking I wouldn't get out, not yet. For getting out would only mean roaming again, without purpose or friends, homeless and lonely. In Walden City I at least had a job and saw faces to which I could attach names.

And so I stayed on. If I had known how much trouble staying on was going to bring me, I wouldn't have done it.

Big Jim was even uglier up close than he had been at a distance. But there was nothing ugly about the way he handled a deck of cards. Those big fingers bent and flexed with the limber beauty of snakes, making the cards move and shuffle with the precision of soldiers.

The game was faro, my weakest weakness. Too bad for me, because a skilled dealer, the sole handler of the cards in this particular game, could clean out a faro player's purse quicker than a London pickpocket. And Big Jim the Scarnose had every appearance of being a skilled dealer.

Or maybe I was just edgy, sitting there in the crowded saloon, violating one of the fundamental rules of my employment because I didn't have the fortitude to say no. I was no better than Fiddler Smith, when it came down to it. The only difference was our weaknesses, his being whiskey and Vera Ann Walden, mine being the gaming table.

The outcome of faro is staked on the order of appearance of certain cards, and my prognostication skills obviously were no match for Big Jim's dealing. "I'm out," I said in disgust after losing yet again. Standing, I pushed back my chair.

"Hey," Big Jim said. "You—somebody said you were law in Walden City."

"Who said that?" I demanded, acting offended. I didn't want this man to learn the truth.

"Don't matter. Are you law?"

"I don't believe a good man of Ike Walden's

kind of law would be playing faro in a saloon, do you?"

He didn't answer me. Those dark eyes cut another couple of holes through me and then lowered to the cards again. I pushed my way through the crowd, heading for the door and fresh air. The stench of tobacco and unwashed miners made it hard to breathe the saloon air for too long at a stretch.

Outside the air was much cleaner. I rolled a smoke and grinned up at the sign above the big front door. Big Jim's partner, a weasly little British scrapper who sported arm garters and the mouth-filling name of Alphonzo M. Swallows-Beasley, had tauntingly named the establishment King Ike's. Ike Walden was reportedly appropriately furious.

"Nice-looking sign, don't you think?"

It was Tate Baker, a beer in his hand and grin on his face. "You have a way of coming up unexpected on a man," I commented.

"I find being lightfooted is a valuable trait to cultivate, particularly when one has to beat a hasty departure."

"You have much experience with hasty departures, Baker?"

"The question is whether you have, McCan." He became just a touch more serious. "The proprietors here don't much like you hanging around. They think you're in here spying for Ike Walden."

I laughed at that one. "If Walden knew I was here, he'd have my backside."

"He's bound to find out—folks know you."

"Let him find out. I don't care."

"You talk just like your fiddle-playing boss."

"When did you talk to Fiddler?"

"Earlier this evening. He was right over there putting away whiskey like it was water. He's not too friendly a sort, is he?"

That didn't sound like the Fiddler I knew. "Usually he's as friendly as they come."

"That right? Well, he must have something on his mind, then. He was cussing everything and everybody when I was around him. Mostly he was cussing Ike Walden, and talking about getting shut of him." Baker leaned over a little, dropping his voice. "You know what folks say? They say that Fiddler Smith and Ike Walden's girl have something going. Not that that would be any big surprise. That Vera Ann Walden is a bit too free with the menfolk."

Obviously Baker hadn't seen me during my little forced outing with Vera Ann; otherwise he wouldn't have dared speak so freely about her.

"So Fiddler Smith isn't her first . . . conquest?"

"Not by a long shot. No sir."

"That's interesting," I said thoughtfully. "Mighty interesting."

Fiddler was scraping out a slowed-down Irish reel on his rosin-caked fiddle when I came in later that night. He looked somewhat ashen and wasn't his usual jubilant self.

"You feeling all right, Fiddler?"

He put down his fiddle and stared at the scroll of it, lightly plucking at the E string with his forefinger. "You're looking at a man with a lot to mull," he said.

"Vera Ann?"

He nodded.

"Is she . . ."

"Yes. She's pregnant." He let out a loud sigh. "I ain't never fathered a baby before. Didn't aim to now."

I cleared my throat. What I had to say might not be taken well. "You might not be the father, Fiddler."

He looked up at me curiously, that expression giving way to one of anger as he understood my implication. "You watch what you say about my woman, McCan!"

"It ain't what I say, it's what others tell me. Apparently Vera Ann has a . . . history, if you follow me. Look now, Fiddler, don't get mad—this is just what I hear on the streets."

"In the gutters is more like it!"

"Hear me out—you owe it to yourself to listen. Fiddler, I think Vera Ann may have already been pregnant before she ever took up with you. She's looking for a way out of Walden City before her father catches on to her condition." I paused. "She even tried to talk me into taking her away myself."

He rose and came at me, his fiddle falling from his lap to the floor. I deflected his fist and got a grip on his arm. He was too drunk to put up any kind of fight.

"Dang it, Fiddler, calm down! I'm saying what I'm saying because I owe it to you as a friend."

"Friend? What kind of friend spreads such truck about a man's woman?"

"I'm sorry. I just don't want you to get bumfuzzled into something you'll regret later. You got to consider the strong possibility that Vera Ann is just looking for somebody to take care of her and get her away from that lead-weight father of hers."

Fiddler was getting green around the edges now

and staggered away from me, trying to hold down the contents of his stomach. A minute or two later he seemed back in control of both his belly and his emotions.

"I'll overlook what you said, McCan, because I like you. But I don't believe you. Vera Ann says I'm the father of that baby, and I don't think she's a liar."

He sat down again and checked his fiddle to make sure it hadn't been damaged when it fell. Satisfied, he took it to his bed and put it into its flour sack.

"I'm taking her away from here, right after I get paid," he said. "That means the law job will be yours to do alone. Maybe Walden will let you hire you some help."

"Maybe. If I stay around."

"You thinking of leaving? You could go off with Vera Ann and me—long as you watch your mouth. We're going up to your old stomping grounds, Montana. I want Vera Ann to meet that brother of mine in Powderville."

"Thanks, but no thanks. I'll go . . . somewhere. Don't know where. Don't know when, either. Since the saloon opened the place is a bit more interesting."

"Ain't that the truth. I been in there myself, you know."

"So I heard. Hey, did you see the Indian?"

Fiddler looked at me quizzically. "No—what Indian?"

"One of the proprietors. Big and ugly and scarred, and he's missing an ear, just like you. Except he doesn't cover his with a patch. Tonight he dealt faro and I . . . Fiddler, what's wrong?"

He looked sick again, worse than before. He staggered back to his bed and sat down, hand on stomach.

"What's wrong with you?"

He shook his head. "Too much to drink, that's all." Rising, he lurched past me and out the door.

Chapter 7

I dreamed of Cynthia, alive and married to me. It was early morning of a bright spring day, the smell of frying bacon filled our house, and she was delicate and beautiful as she walked in and touched me to wake me and tell me breakfast was waiting . . .

Except Cynthia would never have shaken me this roughly. Nor would she have reeked of whiskey and pipe smoke. I sat up, my wonderful dream giving way to the dull reality of the Walden City hut, and Fiddler Smith's unshaven face hovering above me.

"Get up, McCan," he said tersely. "We got a job to do."

I blinked, fumbling for lamp and matches. "A job? What time is it?"

"Three o'clock the morning after payday, that's what," he said. "Now get up—Walden's give us a job."

"At this time of night? What kind of job is it?"

"Just get up and shut up. I've already got the horses saddled and waiting."

My mind was so bleary I wondered if this was

nothing but a dream after all. Maybe the earlier part about marriage to Cynthia was the reality and this was the fantasy, the nightmare.

If only it could really be like that.

Fiddler had two jugs tied together and slung over the back of his horse. I asked what they were, but he didn't answer. His manner was intense, determined, unspeaking. A very bad feeling began to come over me.

We rode through the sleeping town—in liquorless, cardless Walden City, there was nothing to keep most people up late—and out onto the new but well-beaten trail toward the saloon. The farther we rode the more my feeling of disquiet grew.

"Fiddler, just what are we about to do?"

"Shut up and ride. Don't make noise."

"What the devil are we doing?"

"A job for Walden—that's all you need to know."

The saloon was open. There were several horses and wagons outside it even at this hour.

"I don't like this, Fiddler. What are we up to?"

Fiddler was breathing loudly through his nostrils, his lips clamped tightly shut. I hadn't seen him like this before. He led us to a thicket near the saloon and dismounted. I remained in the saddle for a few moments, considering whether I should turn and ride away. Everything about Fiddler's manner smacked of trouble.

"Get down off that horse, McCan," he said gruffly.

Had I disobeyed him at that point and gotten away from there, it would have been the wisest thing. That's hindsight, though, and as you know, hindsight usually finds itself looking back on mistakes. I dismounted as instructed.

Fiddler pulled the twin jugs off his saddle. He moved quickly, fiercely. I swear I could almost hear the pounding of his heart from where I stood. Or maybe it was mine.

"Seems a peculiar time to be taking a drink," I said.

He popped the cork. A breeze wafted across us, carrying the smell of the bottle's contents. Kerosene.

Fiddler's intentions needed no explaining now. He had come here, and dragged me with him, to burn down a saloon. A saloon with patrons still inside. Ike Walden obviously had concluded his problem required a radical solution.

But it was a solution I would be no part of.

"No, Fiddler," I said. "This is loco—we can't set fire to a building, I don't care who ordered it! Walden's a crazy man. In the name of heaven, Fiddler, somebody might die in there!"

"Hell, they'll get out—there's a big door, ain't there? You turning yellow all at once, McCan? Scared to do your job? You damn sure ain't backed down on Walden's orders before! You've kissed his feet, trying to climb up over me so he'd favor you! I know he's took to paying you near as much as me. Trying to get my job, that's what you've been up to!"

I couldn't believe what I was hearing. Was this the same man who had told me he was handing over his job to me, without me even asking for it, so he could run off with his woman? I saw now that Fiddler had been secretly jealous of me, probably stemming from the way I had risen in Ike

Walden's eyes even as he had declined. That's a funny thing about some people: they care deeply about what others think of them, even those they despise.

"I'm not after your job, Fiddler. I don't want your job. God only knows why I've been fool enough to keep my own this long. I'm through— I'll have nothing to do with torching a building."

I guess it was the whiskey and anger mixing together inside him that made him lose his control and swing the jug at me. It was made of heavy crockery and hit my skull like rock. I went down, groped upward through the stars and rockets that exploded and flared a foot above me, then passed out cold.

Cold water splashed my face and washed the blackness away. My eyes opened and were confused by a yellow-orange glow that bathed the tall figures above me. I seemed to be in the bottom of a grave, looking up at the mourners who surrounded me, grief on their torchlit faces.

Then understanding began to return. I lay not in a grave, but on the ground. The men gathered around me were not mourners; what I had seen as expressions of grief were actually looks of deep anger. And the yellow glow was not torchlight. It came from the flaming saloon.

"Oh, no," I murmured. "He went and did it."

"What'd he say?" one of the men above me asked. A face descended, drawing near mine. It was Swallows-Beasley, the Britisher.

"What do you have to say for yourself, you bloody arsonist!" his crisply accented voice said.

"Fiddler . . ."

"Eh? What's that?"

"Fiddler . . . where's Fiddler?"

One of the others said, "He's talking about Fiddler Smith, Ike Walden's marshal. Now I know this bird—his name's McCan. He's a marshal, too, or a deputy."

"Do tell! Well, soon he'll be nothing but a corpse on the end of a rope." He leaned even closer. His breath stunk in my nostrils. "Talk to me, McCan. Did Ike Walden order my saloon burned?"

"Get . . . out of my face . . ."

He struck me, sending up stars again. This time I remained conscious. "Don't talk smart with me, McCan. You can make this a lot easier on yourself by speaking up—or else I'll turn you over to my red-skinned partner for his own brand of persuasion."

My eyes shifted; now I saw the wide, scarred face of Big Jim glaring down at me. Satan himself couldn't have been uglier.

"I didn't burn your saloon," I said weakly.

"No? So it sparked up all of itself, then? You expect me to believe that?" Swallows-Beasley said.

I forced myself to think—I had to find some way out of a lynchman's noose. "I didn't burn your saloon," I reaffirmed. "But I saw the man who did . . . he hit me when I came after him."

"Is that so? And why, pray tell, would a peace officer with no authority outside Walden City be prowling about all the way out here in the middle of the night?"

"I was coming for a drink. I've been here before."

"That's true," someone said. "I seen him at the faro table. You dealt his game, Big Jim."

The Indian said something that reached me only as a bearish growl.

"I don't believe you, McCan," Swallows-Beasley said. "You smell too strong of kerosene for me to buy that bill of goods."

Kerosene . . . indeed I did smell it hanging about me. I remembered the crockery jug. Probably it had cracked when it struck my skull. Some of its contents must have spilled on me.

Fiddler . . . where was he? Why had he abandoned me here to be found by these men? It was equivalent to leaving me to die.

Anger surged and gave me strength. My fist came up and pounded Swallows-Beasley, making him grunt and jerk back. I rose, but found the world spinning around me. Something encircled my neck—an arm, a massive arm. Big Jim the Scarnose had me firmly in his grasp. I gasped for air that would not come.

"No, not that way!" Swallows-Beasley said, rubbing his chin. "We'll swing him properly—with Ike Walden right beside him."

The statement drew a roar of assent from the saloon's former patrons. Fiddler's firing of the saloon had roused a lynch-mob fury among these men, many of whom were on the outs with the oppressive Walden anyway. The destruction of the saloon was to them a justification for counteraction.

They hustled me toward a rude toolshed that had been nailed together during the saloon's construction and not yet torn down. There was nothing in it now but trash and scraps of wood. Big Jim heaved me inside like I was no heavier than a feather pillow. My head struck the wall when I fell to the dirt floor, and I sank down, not unconscious but slightly stunned. Light from the burning saloon probed through cracks and knotholes in the board walls.

Outside the mob was growing louder, rowdier. They were a pack of dogs who had tasted blood and were thirsty for more. In the tangle of words pouring from them I heard eager talk of hanging Ike Walden. The level of tension and anger in the atmosphere was too high to let me believe the threat was idle. In minutes this mob would move through the night to Walden City, and bring back Ike Walden with them. I doubted anyone would dare try to stop them. Walden would hang with me right beside him.

I rolled over and groaned. Right then I could have killed Fiddler Smith with my own hands, for this was his fault entirely.

Part of me wanted to pound on the shed door and shout out that the man who really deserved to hang was Fiddler Smith, not me. It was Fiddler who had actually done the deed, Fiddler who had left me helpless, to be found and charged the price of a crime that had not been mine.

But I didn't do it. Maybe it was because I was too honorable. Or maybe just too stunned.

Chapter 8

Through a knothole I watched the mob recede toward Walden City. To my dismay, though not to my surprise, they left two men to guard me, figuring, I guess, that I might be able to pound my way out of so crude a shed if left alone.

I sat alone in the dark little shack, my face pressed against the knothole, wildly searching for a plan to get me out of here. My two guards were drunk, and after the mob went out of sight, they turned their attention to watching the spectacular destruction of the saloon. The fire was at its peak now, pouring enough light through the cracks of my shed to let me see fairly well. The heat of the blaze was tremendous, even as far from it as I was.

Heaven above, how my head hurt! I rubbed it gently, rolling my neck in a vain attempt to lessen the throbbing. In a few moments I gave it up. What would it matter how my head felt when they put that noose around my neck?

A fierce defiance sparked in me. No. I wouldn't stand by, waiting for a gaggle of drunks to end my life. I would fight to the end—no, until the end was avoided. There in that shed I learned something about myself: Despite all my despair at the loss of Cynthia, despite my foolish and self-destructive gambling and drifting, despite my occasional assertions to myself that life didn't matter anymore . . . despite all these things, I wanted to live. I wanted to see the morning and breathe the air and know what it was like to grow old, even if I grew old alone.

Surely there was something here to use as a weapon. If I was to escape, it must be soon, before the mob returned. Against two men I stood a slim chance; against a full mob I stood none.

Dropping to my knees, I felt about the shed floor. Nothing. Papers, bent nails, empty boxes. Despair began to mount. Then one of the walls of the burning saloon crashed in, sending up an explosion of sparks and intensified light that spilled through the shed walls and revealed something standing in the corner. An ax.

I leaped up and grabbed it. My heart sank. This wasn't an ax, just an ax handle, and broken at that. What could I do with this? I noted the broken end was splintered to a point. A man could gore another man with that—but not with a wall dividing them.

I had to get out of the shed somehow. Setting the ax handle aside for a moment, I began examining the walls. They were rough, splintered, haphazard, but strong. I did not find a single board loose enough for me to kick away, not without raising a major ruckus.

Well, maybe that's what I would just have to do. If I made enough trouble, the two guards would have to open the door to come in and stop me. A well-timed thrust or two with the splintered ax handle might, just might, be enough to get me past them. Then I could run into the forest as far as I could and escape them. Yes sir, if I could only get to the forest, escape I would. I'd run all the way to Mexico if I had to.

Locating what looked like the weakest wallboard, I raised my foot to pound at it. Before I could, one of the men outside shouted to the other, who apparently had wandered off some distance, "Hey, Big Jim's coming back!"

That stopped me. I went back to my knothole at once. Sure enough, the hulking Indian was riding back into the wide circle of firelight. My guards stepped forward to meet him. Fortunately, they came together while still within my earshot.

"You forget something, Big Jim?"

"No. Swallows-Beasley sent me back. Change of plans. I came back to get this McCan. We'll take him into Walden City and hang him there with Walden. We don't want to have to drag Walden all the way back here before we lynch him."

"Well, that makes sense," one of them said. "Let's hurry—I don't want to miss seeing Walden hang."

Big Jim dismounted and strode toward the shed. I took a dry swallow, picked up my ax handle, and readied myself for the opening of the door.

The Indian let out a yell when the sharp point probed into his broad midsection. It didn't poke deep, but splintered off and remained stuck into him an inch or so. I bounded right over him, leapfrogging like I had done with friends back in my Missouri boyhood. The two surprised guards let out a shout and came at me, tugging at pistols. I yelled right back, like the Rebel soldiers used to do, and came at the nearest one with the ax handle extended. He ducked to the side and missed the thrust. It didn't help him much, because I brought the ax handle down like a club and caught him on the back of the head. He fell with a loud grunt.

The other guard had his pistol out by now but was too unnerved to fire. I ran straight at him and hit him on the side of the head. He fell to his knees. I grabbed his pistol.

Now there was more than just hope. I had a weapon.

Big Jim's horse stood where he had left it, and I ran straight for it and leaped into the saddle from behind like the finest dime-novel hero you ever read about. I had tried to do that sometimes, just fooling around back in my earlier cowpoke days, and had never achieved it nearly so well as now. I felt proud of myself.

The feeling was short-lived. Big hands came up from the side and grabbed my clothes. I was pulled from the saddle before I knew what was happening.

It was Big Jim, of course. He threw me aside; I hit the ground and rolled. To my good fortune I kept hold of the pistol, which I swung up and fired, twice. Both shots went high. I squeezed the trigger a third time and nothing happened. The gun had been loaded with only two cartridges.

Big Jim grinned and bore down on me. I scrambled to my feet and tried to dart away, but he had me. I fell and he was there, leaning over me with that fierce grin burning down from his ugly face.

"Now, McCan, you talk to me! They said you called the name Fiddler before I came up close enough to hear. They tell me this Fiddler is the marshal of Walden City, and you help him. You tell me: Does he have only one ear, like me?"

"Yes," I said. "Yes . . . one ear."

His face was even uglier after that. Another wall of the saloon crashed in and sent up more sparks, light, and heat. Big Jim shook me, knocking the back of my head against the ground.

"Fiddler Smith! Fiddler Smith is here?"

I remembered now how Fiddler had gone pale the time I mentioned the big, one-eared Indian who ran the saloon. These two must have had more in common than missing ears. They had histories that overlapped, and apparently not pleasantly.

"I'll kill him!" he said in a fierce and triumphant tone. "At last I'll kill him, kill him dead!"

It came to me that I still had the pistol in my hand. It was empty but heavy. I brought up my arm as hard as I could and let the blue steel barrel say a firm hello to the side of Big Jim's head.

What happened next was so rushed and confused that I can't fully describe it. Somehow I was up again, Big Jim grappling at me. One of the men who had guarded me joined him, but tripped up and wound up getting in Big Jim's way instead of helping. At the same time, the lynch mob came riding back in, drawn back by the sound of my two earlier gunshots. I ran, they pursued. The woods loomed dark before me, then swallowed me. I dodged through brush and clambered across rocks and ravines.

They could not ride here, and so came on foot. Their voices were loud behind me, and too close. My head hurt worse than ever. The land tilted up before me and I climbed, straining for breath. I reached the top of a ridge, but my foot caught on a root. With an involuntary yell I fell, tumbling into a ravine. At the bottom I lay still, unable to rise. I was on my back, looking up at the sky.

They were close now; their voices were louder by the moment and rising toward the crest from which I had fallen. Groaning, I tried to rise again and managed only to push up onto my elbows. Maybe they would pass me by. Maybe they wouldn't see the ravine . . .

Then a face appeared, looking down over the edge of the ravine. It was dark and I could see no features, just the outline of the shape. I froze in place, hoping that the night shadows would hide me. A moment later a light flared; the man had struck a match.

The matchlight flashed onto the face of Tate Baker. None of it, as I could tell, spilled down on me. The flame held for only a moment before the wind snuffed it.

"Find something, Tate?" someone asked.

There was only the briefest pause before he answered. "Not a thing. He didn't come this way, that's for sure."

After that the voices began to recede. I was alone and alive, and the prayer of thanks I sent up toward the black heavens was surely the most sincere ever voiced by any member of our mortal race.

How long I lay there I'm not sure, but it couldn't have been long. Though I had momentarily escaped the noose, danger still threatened Ike Walden. I expected that the lynch mob, having given up on me, would now return its attention to finding Walden. He had to be warned, had to know that his order to burn the saloon that mocked his name and his philosophy was about to cost him dear.

I climbed out of the ravine and headed down

through the forest, aiming for the trail to Walden City. It felt as if a great weight rested on my shoulders, the combined result of injury, weariness, and the need to reach Walden before the lynch mob did. I reached the trail to Walden City and discovered, from hearing their noise beyond me, that the lynchmen had already passed. I could not hope to make it to Walden City before them—unless I could take a shorter route by leaving the trail.

Such a thing was possible, for the trail curved and followed the easiest portions of the terrain. As the crow flies, the distance to Walden's "palace" was much shorter. Too bad I wasn't a crow.

If I couldn't fly, at least I could attempt to maneuver a more direct route by land. The effort seemed doomed, but if following the trail was obviously hopeless, what harm could come from trying the only alternative?

So into the forest on the other side of the trail I went. I knew the general direction toward Walden's house and tried to keep on that line as closely as possible. The darkness was thick here and had me groping like a blind man. I had almost given up the effort as failed when I emerged into the clearing on the hillside where Walden's big house stood.

Pausing, panting for breath, I listened. Distantly I heard the sound of the mob. They would be here within minutes.

No time to waste. As quickly as I could, I half-ran, half-staggered around to the front of Walden's house. I pounded the door and shouted for entry. A few moments later the door opened slowly.

Ike Walden, lamp in hand, faced me. His face was white and his hair mussed, his clothing disheveled.

He looked so bad that for a couple of seconds I forgot the urgent matter that had led me here.

"Mr. Walden, are you sick?"

He looked at me with lusterless eyes. "Vera Ann is gone," he said. "She's gotten herself pregnant and made me give her money and now she's gone, run off with her man."

"Her man?"

"Yes . . . she's run off with Fiddler Smith."

Chapter 9

Walden slumped back toward a chair that sat beside an end table in his front parlor and plopped heavily into it. The lamp he sat on the floor beside his bare feet. He stared into a corner like he was drugged. My eyes flicked over to the little table and saw a bottle and glass. Now I really was amazed. Ike Walden, champion of temperance, was drinking.

"Mr. Walden, you've got to get away from here," I said. "There's a mob coming from the saloon—they plan to hang you for ordering the place burned."

He looked up dully at me. "Burned? I didn't order anything burned."

I let that sink in for a second. "Then it was Fiddler, acting on his own . . . because of Big Jim, no doubt."

None of that made sense to Walden. He lifted the glass and took a swallow of liquor. You would think that a man unaccustomed to alcohol would flinch to swallow as much as Walden did, Walden didn't flinch. Clearly he, like Fiddler Smith, had been drinking on the sneak a long time. It was one of the most ironic revelations of my life.

"Coming to hang me," he repeated calmly. For some reason he chuckled. "Coming to hang me."

"They would have hung me, too, if I hadn't got loose," I said. "Come on, Mr. Walden, let's get you out of here."

He said and did nothing for several seconds. Off in the distance I heard disturbing sounds. I could feel the mob's approach even without seeing it. Suddenly Ike Walden violently swept his arm across the table, upsetting it, spilling the bottle and glass across the carpet. He stood, wobbling a little.

"Coming to hang me, are they? Hell, I'll be ready for 'em!"

He stomped over to a cabinet, pulled open the door, and brought out a long old shotgun. This he loaded clumsily with shells from a box up on a shelf. "Let 'em come," he kept repeating over and over. "Let 'em come."

"This is insane, Mr. Walden," I said. "You can't hold off a mob with a shotgun. We get you away from here and give this thing time to cool down. That's the thing to do."

"Let 'em come—I'll blow their skulls open. Then it'll be Fiddler Smith's turn."

What a time for Ike Walden to get liquored up and loco! It was all I could do to keep my feet, for I ached and throbbed from my own ordeal and scramble through the forest. I was in no shape at the moment to physically force Ike Walden to come with me—and it appeared that physical force would be the only thing that would break his resolution.

I stepped forward. "Mr. Walden, I insist that

you come with me. Listen—can you hear them coming?''

He turned a cold gaze on me. "You're my employee, McCan—you do what I tell you, not the other way around.''

"You're in no condition to make decisions, Mr. Walden. You're drunk.''

You should have seen how his eyes fired at that. A more fierce face you wouldn't expect to find under an executioner's cowl. "You're accusing me of drunkenness?'' he bellowed. "You're accusing *me*?''

"Calm down, Mr. Walden . . .''

"There's a rifle in the cabinet—get it and ready it, McCan.''

"Mr. Walden, if you don't come with me I'll have to use force.''

"I told you to ready that rifle, McCan! We have a fight ahead!''

"No—no fight. We've got to get away from here.''

"You're a coward, McCan. I despise cowards.'' And with that he swung up the shotgun and brought the butt of it arcing around toward my head. Under normal circumstances I could have ducked it, but in the shape I was then my reflexes were rusty. The hard buttplate struck my skull and drove me down. Unconsciousness came immediately.

The smell of smoke was choking and acrid when I came to. This wasn't the hot smoke of a blazing fire but the searing, thick kind that pours from something smoldering. I sat up, groaning, and found myself still in Walden's front parlor. The house was filled with smoke. Coughing, I stood.

"Mr. Walden!" I yelled as best my smoke-tightened throat would allow. "Mr. Walden, where are you?"

I found the source of the smoke—a pile of rags and such in the sitting room. Somebody had set the things afire, but they hadn't fully caught. Certainly someone in the saloon mob had done it—and it chilled me to know they surely had known I was lying unconscious in the very house they had set out to burn. I suppose it was my anticipated death by burning that had saved me from lynching.

"Mr. Walden!" I yelled again. No answer in the house . . . but I became conscious of frightening and distant sounds outside. I went to a window.

Walden City was burning. Not the whole town, but at least half of it, with the rest bound to catch. In the streets, lit now by the several blazes, I saw riders and runners all about, torches waving, guns firing into the sky. The saloon mob was avenging itself brutally against Walden's perceived attack. I prayed no innocent townsman had died in the tumult.

"Fiddler Smith, this is on your head," I said aloud in the dark room.

In all my life there were few, if any, times that I felt as helpless as at that moment. Down below me a town I had been hired to protect was being ravaged. Yet what could I, a lone man, do about it?

I had to do something, had to try. Heading back to the cabinet, I found the rifle, a Winchester, that Walden had mentioned, and two boxes of ammunition. I loaded the rifle, pocketed the rest of the cartridges, and headed out.

I didn't make it down the hill to the edge of

town before I found Walden. He lay on the muddy road, face down, a wide puddle of red beneath him. Touching his back, I found no movement of heart or breath. His shotgun was still gripped in his hand. Both barrels had been emptied.

I had never felt any affection for Walden, but right then I could have cried for him. The pompous man with his big ideas and big utopian dreams had come to a sad and ignoble end, his town being destroyed before him, his pride-and-joy daughter run off with a man who had betrayed Walden's trust and encouraged his daughter to betray him, too.

Finding Walden's body drained me of my impulse to respond to the carnage in the streets below. I turned and plodded back up the hill and around to Walden's little stable. There I took a horse and saddle, mounted, and rode off. The night was nearly spent; in an hour the sun would rise and spill its light onto the smoking shell of Ike Walden's dear departed dream. And when that happened, I didn't plan to be around to see it.

The sun, run by those universal clockwork gears that keep working in peaceful ignorance of the doings of the wicked creature, man, lit the Colorado landscape, but not my spirits. I had put three miles between me and Walden City before I finally reined to a halt and twisted in my saddle to look behind. Smoke billowed into the morning sky. I sighed, turned the horse, and began plodding back.

I wasn't sure why I felt compelled to return. Maybe it was duty. Maybe it was curiosity, having to know what the outcome of the Walden City attack had been. Or maybe it was the need to make firm my own case against Fiddler Smith and Vera

Ann Walden, whose combined irresponsibility was the spark that had fired this tragedy.

What was left of Walden City wasn't much to look at. The fire had spread since I had left and even now was finishing off several sheds and outbuildings. Most of the main buildings had been destroyed. Only a handful of sizable structures had been saved.

I rode down the center of the street. The people of Walden City stood, stared, paced, murmured. There was a tangible feeling of general disbelief. And well there should be. How many of these people even yet knew what had caused the mob to destroy their town? The average Walden City resident knew nothing of the saloon-burning that had led to this.

An armed man, followed by three others, strode up to me. I stopped my horse and stared down at him. He was Joe Gamble, a dry-goods merchant of good reputation in the town. I glanced past him to where his store had stood. It was a smoking ruin of black lumber.

"Mr. McCan, I strongly suggest you turn that horse around and get out of this town right away," Gamble said.

I lifted my left brow. "I gather I'm not held in high esteem here, eh?"

Gamble apparently thought I was trying to make a joke, and it made him mad. "Damn it, McCan, we could string you up right here on the street and be within our rights to do it. This is your fault, yours and that worthless superior of yours."

"Fiddler Smith's fault, yes. Mine, no."

"You're trying to say you didn't help torch that saloon?"

"So you've found out about that, huh? No, I didn't. In fact, I objected and got myself knocked cold by Fiddler Smith for my trouble. I near got myself hung, too. Not that you're going to believe a word I say."

"Was it Walden who ordered the saloon burned?"

"That's what Fiddler said, though Walden denied it. I believe Walden."

Gamble snorted. "Walden will get his chance to explain himself."

"He's unavailable. Off meeting the maker he didn't believe in."

Gamble cocked his head. "Are you saying he's dead?"

"Yep—up on the track to his house. Shot to death. I found him before dawn."

Gamble stared up at me as if he was considering gunning me right out of my saddle. I could hardly blame him. Fiddler had left me in a bad situation.

"I'd like to ride out of here," I said to Gamble.

He thought about it a couple of moments, then nodded tersely. I turned the horse and plodded away, heading for the edge of town. I knew I would never again return to Walden City, but I didn't have even the slightest impulse to look back.

Chapter 10

After three hours of riding, weariness caught up with me and I began to think about stopping to sleep. I kept putting it off, though; the more distance between me and Walden City, the better. Fort Collins was my destination—it was about the only place I could handily reach from Walden City. Where I was going after Fort Collins I didn't know; all that mattered was going, and putting behind me all the bad things that had come of taking up with Fiddler Smith.

I thought about Fiddler as my horse loped along, and the more I thought the madder I got. He had been trouble from the first moment I laid eyes on him in that Nebraska saloon. Thanks to him I had taken a trouncing there, and now, again thanks to him, I had barely escaped being lynched first by a saloon mob, then by the very townspeople I had tried to help. Yes sir, I owed Fiddler Smith quite a lot.

The most maddening thing of all was that he had left me there at that burning saloon—left me, senseless and defenseless, to take the blame for what he had done. Could that have been his very reason for taking me there in the first place—to be his scapegoat? Maybe it was jealousy over Vera Ann's interest in me. I didn't like to think of Fiddler as so low a sort . . . but maybe he was.

I thought about trying to track him down and settle my accounts with him . . . but no. It really wasn't worth it. I would just count myself lucky to be alive and put my association with Fiddler down to bad experience. Bad—but interesting. That much I had to admit.

Ahead of me on the trail I saw a rider. His tracks had been clear on the earth before me since I had crossed the Walden City limit. I had crossed the first person abandoning the town. Likely I wouldn't be the last, either. Lots of folks would decline to hang around after such a tragedy. And when the town rebuilt, it would probably be a far different place than when Ike Walden governed it. Without his strong personality in charge, all his ''scientific'' moralisms would die away. Whatever new Walden City phoenixed out of the old one's ashes would surely include saloons and faro parlors and houses of ill repute. Churches, too. All the things Ike Walden wanted to avoid. The town would thrive and shine and attract both those wanting a foothold and those wanting to be footloose, and eventually it would die and rot away into the Colorado mountain soil. Such was the way of so many mining camps of the day.

At length I caught up with the rider ahead of me, and found it was Tate Baker. The realization was startling, for Baker had been among the saloon mob who chased me up into the forest. I decided a quiet retreat was in order.

Too late. Baker, who was sitting under a tree

eating beans from a can, looked up and saw me.
He stood quickly—too quickly. The rifle I had
taken from Walden's was slung by a cord over the
saddle horn; I grabbed it and swung it free and
upward, leveling it on Baker.

"Luke McCan, is that any way to treat the man
who saved your neck from the noose?" he said,
lifting his hands.

I lowered the rifle a little. "You mean you saw
me in that gully?"

"Sure did. And if you'll recall, it was me who
turned them off in the wrong direction so you could
stay alive. Dang, McCan, the only reason I went
after you with that rabble was to try to save your
skin!"

He was sincere and his story rang true. I decided
to believe him and rebooted the rifle. "All right.
You'll pardon me for being uncertain."

"Sure I will. I'd be jumpy, too, in your boots.
Come on over here and have some beans with me.
Man, you look a sight!"

"Rough night."

"Don't I know it."

He pulled another can of beans from his pack,
opened it, and handed it to me, along with a rusty
spoon. Because of how busy and tense the past several hours had been, I had overlooked my own hunger. The beans disappeared rapidly and left me
scraping the juices from the bottom of the can.

Baker talked as I ate. He was leaving Walden
City, like I was, largely in disgust. He had been
ready to go at any point, anyway; all the trouble of
the previous night had been the final nudge. He had
simply mounted and ridden out before dawn.

His talk turned back to the beginning of the

night's trouble. He had been in the saloon, he said, when it was first torched. One wall was well ablaze before anyone inside realized it; all efforts to save it failed.

Baker described his own mounting fears as the realization spread among the saloon patrons that the fire had been deliberately set. "They all blamed Ike Walden," he said. "No one doubted for a minute that he had been the one behind it. When they started talking about lynching, I decided to get out—and then they found you. I stayed around, figuring you would need some help getting out of that particular jam."

Once I was locked up in the shed, Baker told me, he had gone on with the mob toward Walden City, hoping he could cut ahead and give warning to Walden, then rally help in saving me. He had changed that plan when he saw Big Jim turn and ride back toward where I was held; Baker had quietly followed. Then, shortly after, the gunshots had sounded and the entire lynch mob had returned, figuring I was making a break.

"When you headed up into the woods, I hoped to high heaven that I would find you before somebody else did. I'm glad I did, and sorry for all the scare you had."

"All's well that ends well, as they say," I replied. "For a while there I thought Big Jim was going to have my hide."

"Well, tell me straight, McCan, did you help torch the saloon?"

"No. It was Fiddler Smith all the way. And Ike Walden didn't order it, either; Fiddler did it on his own. I think it was because of this Big Jim character."

"What do you mean?"

"Big Jim knows Fiddler somehow, and vice versa. There's no love lost between them. When Big Jim left that mob to come back to me, it was Fiddler he asked about. He wanted him, bad."

"Now, that's a strange thing," Baker said. "And this ain't the first I've heard of it. I'd picked up word already that Big Jim was acquainted with our good town marshal. I'd sure like to know the story behind it." He lit a cigar stub he dug from a pocket. "Like to know it, but don't. I can tell you some more about Big Jim, though. I picked up some on him since we last talked."

"Like what?"

"Like how he lost that ear. It was back in '79, in the North Park area. You ever heard of the Independent Army?"

I had and told him so. The Independent Army was the overgrandiose name given to what amounted to a band of cutthroats hired by the leaders of the Craig City mining town in Colorado's North Park area back in 1879. Led by a fortyish Georgia ruffian named J. D. Reed, a veteran of the Third Georgia Rifles, the Independent Army was established to spook off any troublesome Indians about Craig City. The way they did it was vicious: the Craig Park leadership provided the Independent Army a base pay, supplemented by a bonus for every pair of Cheyenne or Sioux ears turned in. Reed would receive twenty-five dollars for every pair; a like amount would go to whatever Independent Army member actually removed the ears from the victim.

That, at least, was the version of the story I had heard. The end of the story was no prettier than the

beginning. After Reed's "army" began preying on
innocent Indians, including children, a party of
Sioux decided to settle the problem on their own
terms. The bulk of the Independent Army was mas-
sacred and their bodies axed to pieces. Reed suffered badly before his own end; when the Craig
City leadership found him, he was nailed alive to
a tree, with his eyes missing. The Sioux had left
him like that. He was shot to death by his finders
to end his misery. It was a terrible end for the Independent Army. Terrible, though not undeserved,
in my opinion.

"So Big Jim lost that ear to the Independent
Army?" I asked. "I wonder how he managed to
keep the other one?"

"And how he kept his life, too? The only thing
I can figure is he managed to escape whoever sliced
him."

I sat down my empty bean can, thinking. "You
know, Fiddler talked about being at Craig City. I
wonder if he might have been part of the Independent Army. It could explain him and Big Jim
knowing and despising each other."

"It's a funny coincidence, Fiddler and Big Jim
both shy one ear," Baker said.

"That it is, Tate," I replied. "It's like you said,
wouldn't I like to know the story behind that one."

"So why don't you go find Fiddler Smith and
get that story?"

I shook my head. "It ain't worth it. Let Fiddler
Smith go his way and I'll go mine. I'm through
with him."

"That's the attitude to have, I reckon. I can tell
you one that don't share it, though, and that's Big
Jim."

"What do you mean?"

"Last night, during all the rampaging and burning, that Big Jim spent the whole dang time looking for Fiddler Smith. Whatever them two got between them, it ain't sweet. I don't think Big Jim's going to be content to let Fiddler get away with this one."

"Why do you say that?"

"That Englisher partner of his says Big Jim's declared he wants to go after Fiddler and square things up with him."

I whistled. "I wouldn't envy Fiddler having a devil like Big Jim on his tail."

"Maybe it won't come to that. The Englisher wants to just let Fiddler go. Said it wasn't worth the trouble to go after him. I don't know who won the argument. That was the time I was mounting up to leave town."

We rode together the rest of the day and made a common camp that night. It was beans for supper again.

"So where you bound?" Baker asked me.

"That's a better question than I can answer," I replied. "What about you?"

"Texas. I heard there's always good opportunities in Texas."

"Had your fill of mining?"

"It don't take me long to get my fill of most things. Except beans and beer and saloon sweethearts."

"The beans and beer I can take. Right now the sweethearts don't have much appeal to me." I told him about Cynthia, about how her face was the first thing I pictured when I awakened every morning, the image that stayed with me all day, and haunted me when I blew out the lamp at night. Maybe he didn't want to hear it, but I had to talk.

He proved as good a listener as he was a talker. When I was done he told me he was sorry, then offered his advice. "Find yourself another woman, McCan. There's good ones out there; I've come near marrying a couple of them myself. I skittered free at the last minute both times. Don't know if I was lucky." He chuckled. "Likely they were."

I grinned. "You're not a bad sort of fellow, Tate Baker. You remind me of an old friend I had up in Montana. He was a territorial marshal, name of Taylor Longhurst."

"Marshal, huh? Marshals give me the willies."

"Taylor wouldn't. You and him are biscuits from the same pan."

When I turned in that night, I thought about Longhurst. I hadn't seen him in years, not since the Montana days. But I had heard news of him while I was still in Missouri. He had left Montana and headed to Cheyenne, where he reportedly had joined the town marshal's force.

The next morning I knew where I was bound. Cheyenne lay to the north, an easy ride from Fort Collins. I would go there and look up Taylor Longhurst.

Baker and I reached Fort Collins and stayed there a couple of days until my bruises were better and he felt eager to make for Texas. We parted with a handshake and I set out for Wyoming.

Chapter 11

The rooming house stood on a Cheyenne street that was hardly more than an alley. Running it was a slender little woman with gray hair piled high atop her head and held in place with a pearl clip. She had a gentle face that must have been pretty in her youth; now it was lined and weathered, the corners of the narrow mouth stained with snuff. She granted me the privilege of renting from her because I looked like "an upstanding young man," then warned me not to come in drinking or in any way disturb the other borders, most of whom were elderly.

I made my promises and foresaw no trouble in keeping them. There had been a time when I wouldn't have been so confident, a time when liquor held a grip on me almost as strong as that of gambling. With much effort I had wrestled substantially free of alcohol's hold. Gambling was another story. That demon still held me fast.

That was why that within a day of arriving in Cheyenne, I had already located three good gambling halls. I made a trip to the local bank to arrange to draw on some of my dwindling funds on deposit back in Missouri, then set out to see if I could increase my holdings at the tables. As I pen this narrative from the perspective gained over passing years, I'm ashamed to admit my foolishness of those days. The gaming halls have ruined many a good man, and they almost ruined me.

I strode through the dark streets toward the largest of the gambling houses, my appetite whetted for faro. I ended up with poker instead, following an impulse, and as hours rolled by I had much good luck. About midnight I cashed in my chips and headed back toward my room, cheerful and thinking about looking up Taylor Longhurst the next morning. And in fact I would see him, though under circumstances far different than I had planned.

By the time I reached the street fronting the rooming house, I knew I was being followed. Shadowy figures had slipped out of the gambling hall and now crept in the night shadows behind me, drawing steadily nearer. The rooming-house door was inviting, an entrance to refuge. All I had to do was enter and close it behind me, and my followers would fade back into the night.

I didn't enter it. Out of pride, the couple of beers I had drunk, or maybe simple recklessness I decided to face them down. At the door of the rooming house I spun and saw them emerging. Seeing their prey about to disappear had made them reckless, too.

"Evening, gentlemen," I said. "Is there something I can do for you."

The first one drew near. He was tall and broad and had a voice that growled. "You know what we want. Hand it over and there'll be no trouble for you."

"What I won is mine," I replied. "You want it, you'll have to come and get it."

They did come, both at once. I bore no weapon except a folding knife that I slipped from my pocket as I turned. As they advanced I opened it, waved it—then the foolishness of what I was doing struck me and I wished I had just gone inside.

The thought came too late. My knife didn't frighten either man, for they had knives of their own, and bigger. The big one advanced and I slashed at him but missed. His aim was better, cutting a gash on the back of my hand and making me drop my own weapon.

I ducked the next lunge of the knife and by fortune found a brick that had been kicked loose from the flowerbed border in front of the rooming house. It made a wonderful hammer, and the bigger attacker fell back with a curse and a bruised forehead.

The other ducked and lunged, striking me in the middle and doubling me over. He grabbed my brick and threw it aside. For the next minute I was engaged in a fierce wrestling match with the man; his bigger partner still was out of action, swearing and gingerly holding his bashed forehead.

The door behind me opened. One of the elderly residents had heard the scuffling and had come to investigate, carrying an ancient cap-and-ball pistol. He picked a bad time to open the door, for my foe and I were in the process of falling back against it when he did. As a result we fell atop him, knocking him down. He howled; the pistol went off and shattered a chandelier above the long table in the adjacent dining room.

The fight continued only a few moments more,

and resulted in little damage to either me or my enemy. The furniture wasn't as lucky. By the time my
attacker relented and darted out the door, a chair was
broken and a shelf laden with glassware and china
was overturned. I stood panting, sweating, dripping
blood from my cut hand onto the Oriental carpet.
The old woman who ran the boardinghouse was at
the top of the stairs in a flannel nightgown, scream-
ing out her fury.

"Sorry about the damage," I said. "I'll pay for
it."

"Yes sir, you will," she replied. "You'll pay
dear indeed."

This deputy might have been a brother to the one
who gave me such a hard time back in Nebraska
after that saloon brawl in which I defended Fiddler
Smith. Same build, same expression, same attitude.
He had not a trace of sympathy in him.

My hand was swaddled in a bandage ripped
from a bedsheet. Blood was already soaking
through. I sat in the twin of the chair I had destroyed, sullenly listening to the deputy deride me
as a criminal while the boardinghouse woman
walked around the room, making a list of everything broken and a few things that weren't. When
the deputy referred to her as Aunt Harriet, I knew
I was in big trouble.

"Am I going to jail?" I asked.

"He ought to," muttered the old man with the
pistol. He and all the other aging boarders were
standing around looking at me like I was worse
trash than Jesse James.

"Well, sir, that just depends on you. Depends
on your attitude, Mr. McCan." The deputy was

haughtier than Ike Walden had ever thought of being. He said my name like it was a swear word.

"What attitude should I have? I was only defending myself."

"We may just have to let the judge decide that, Mr. McCan."

"Look, if you're asking me to pay for the damages, I've already agreed to that."

"Well, that's the right spirit, Mr. McCan. Pay you will, yes sir." He turned. "Aunt Harriet, how much you figure?"

The old woman, eyes spitting lightning, walked over and plopped down her list in front of me. It featured a long column of figures all added up to a total that bugged my eyes.

"I'm not paying that!" I bellowed. "That's ridiculous!"

"Bad attitude, Mr. McCan," the nephew with the badge said.

"Send him to jail!" the old man with the pistol urged. "Teach him what's what!"

I stood, dug my poker winnings from my pocket, and plopped the roll onto the table. "I think that ought to be plenty to pay for anything damaged."

The deputy picked up the bills, counted them, then handed them to his aunt. "That's short by half," he said. "You got more available?"

I did, considering my bank money back in Missouri, but I wasn't about to tell him about it, much less turn it over. "Like I said, I think that's plenty to cover what I broke."

The old woman picked up a shattered pitcher. "This was my mother's," she said eyes reddening. "It meant so much to me."

Now I was getting too mad for my own good.

"Glue the lousy thing back together, then."

The old woman burst into tears and the deputy turned red. "That's it. Come with me, Mr. McCan."

"I want to see Taylor Longhurst."

He didn't seem to know what to make of me calling the name of a fellow lawman. "You'll meet him, I reckon. He comes on duty in the morning."

"You're locking me up?"

"Indeed I am. Follow me, Mr. McCan, and don't try anything."

"You better hope I don't," I said. "I could bounce your head like a blown-up hog bladder if I had a mind to."

I must have sounded mighty dangerous, because he kept his pistol poked into my back all the way to jail. The old folks followed us out as far as the street and watched us tread off until we were out of sight. I figure I had given them the best entertainment that night that they had seen in years.

The rattling of the cell door awakened me the next morning. I sat up as a lean figure in loose-fitting blue trousers strode in with a food-laden tray. I winced at the sunlight that spread through the single narrow window and into my sleepy eyes.

"Lord, don't you look dangerous!" the tray-bearer said. "Maybe I ought to keep you covered with a shotgun in case you try to trounce me with this china plate. I hear you're murder on china plates and such."

Shaking my head to clear it, I finger-combed my hair and rubbed my face. "Shut up, Longhurst," I grumbled. "The last thing I need is smart-mouthing from you."

Taylor Longhurst sat the tray onto my hard bunk and smirked. "Luke McCan. I always knew I'd run into you again. I didn't figure it being in a cell, though. Since when did you turn desperado? Why, they'll be writing you up in them dime novels before long: 'Luke McCan, Terror of the Boarding-house.'"

The comment didn't strike me all that funny. "It don't seem very nice, making fun of a man who's rode this far just to see an old friend."

"You came to see me? Why, I'm flattered, Luke McCan." He stuck out his hand, putting banter aside. "Good to see you, McCan. I've thought on you a lot these past years."

We shook hands and I managed a smile. "Good to see you, too, Longhurst. How's the deputy business suiting you?"

"I'm giving it up. Two weeks. That's all I got left."

"No fooling?" I picked up my coffee cup and took a welcome sip. Not bad for jail coffee.

"That's right. I'll tell you about it later, after we go."

"You mean I'm a free man? I figured old Aunt Harriet would be pressing to have me put away for life."

"Forget about her—she's satisfied now that she's been paid up."

"Paid up? Last night they told me I was half short on what I gave her."

"You were. I paid the rest."

I laid down the forkful of eggs I had just picked up. "I can't let you do that, Longhurst. Heck, I'll pay the rest. I'm not so mad now."

"Forget about it. I got lots of money now. Inheritance. The proverbial old rich uncle. He built up a good pile and then headed across Jordan and left it all to me not a week ago. I just got word on Monday. My notice went in the same day.''

"So you're taking up a life of ease, huh?''

"Not exactly. I'm going to be a cattleman. From now on I'm wrangling cows instead of criminal types like you.''

"You say the nicest things, Longhurst.''

"Finish that breakfast, McCan, then get out of here and see if you can stay out of trouble until this evening. I'll be through working about six o'clock. I'll buy you a meal. A real one, not this jail victual stuff.'' He turned and left the cell. This time the door stayed open.

"It is good to see you, McCan. Brings back the old Montana days. I'm looking forward to hearing what's happened with you since I seen you last. Six o'clock, hear?''

"Six o'clock.''

He grinned and headed toward the front office.

"Longhurst.''

"Yeah?''

"Thanks.''

He grinned again and strode away, whistling "Soldier's Joy.'' The sun sliced in through the window while I finished my meal, and ten minutes after that I was on the street again, broke, without lodging, but happy. I had a friend again. A real friend, not a betrayer like Fiddler Smith had proven to be. It had been a long time, and it felt good.

Chapter 12

We sat in a little cafe and exchanged stories. Longhurst's was simple: He had wearied of the travel and constant vigil required by his work for the government in Montana and had tossed it aside for the smaller-scale task of Cheyenne peace officer. In that job he had been happy until lately, when the urge for an even greater change of pace came upon him. Then word of his uncle's death arrived, and Taylor Longhurst suddenly had bright new prospects. Montana was calling to him; the idea of becoming a cattleman was growing stronger by the day.

Longhurst listened intently to the story of all that had happened to me since our last parting in Montana, back in my days about Timber Creek. At that time we had been riding together, tracking the outlaw Evan Bridger, Longhurst acting on professional motivations, me on personal ones. There had been a third man with us, too: Caleb Black, my old Deadwood mining partner and a man whose ghost-like pursuit of Bridger, the outlaw who had taken the life of his wife and unborn baby, had even then become legend far beyond the Montana Territory.

Longhurst finally gave up the search for Bridger and returned to Fort Maginnis, leaving me and Black to go on after the outlaw alone. We found him, in the end, and there was gunplay . . . and Evan Bridger died with my bullet in him.

If I had desired notoriety I could have had it. I could have been known across the nation as the man who killed Evan Bridger. But it wouldn't have been true. I never took public credit for Bridger's killing, for I knew that it was Evan Bridger who brought about his own death, who orchestrated it with grim cleverness because no matter how hard he denied his own guilt, the guilt wouldn't quit haunting him.

My Montana days came back clearly as I talked to Taylor Longhurst. I was taken in memory back to the Montana countryside, the Timber Creek Cattle Enterprise, the little community of Upchurch, the big Upchurch Emporium—and to Maggie. Maggie Carrington, cowboy's daughter, child of the high plains, and a woman I had once thought would be my own, until Rodney Upchurch came along and took her away.

Maggie. The name was still magic to me.

I told Longhurst about my homecoming to Missouri, my engagement, bereavement, and return to roaming. I admitted the gambling, the lack of purpose, the waste of my money and time. Longhurst listened and did not judge. He had never been a judgmental man. That was part of the reason I liked him so much. As a lawman he knew better than most that human beings were human beings and no more. He demanded no perfection of them, or of himself. In other words, he was comfortable.

When my story turned to Fiddler Smith and

Walden City, Longhurst's interest doubled. The idea of me as a town deputy seemed to strike him as funny. And he was fascinated by the peculiar characters I had been moving among: Ike Walden, Fiddler, Vera Ann . . . and especially Big Jim the Scarnose Sioux, and his British partner Swallows-Beasley.

"Once you cross the Mississippi, you find all kinds crawling across these plains and mountains," Longhurst said. "I think that's half of what makes this wild country so fine for me, and why I became a peace officer. A man of the law meets more than his share of your interesting types."

"Think you'll be able to abide putting all those interesting types aside to wrangle cattle?"

"You bet. I've put in too many years behind the badge already. Before long the averages are bound to catch up with me. Some drunk will pull a pistol on the sneak, and old Taylor Longhurst will have snorted his last snuff."

Taylor was living in a small rented house on a back lot. It had only two rooms in it with hardly enough space in either for a man to squeeze in among the roaches. There was no question of me sharing that meager space with him . . . but there was a shed out back occupied only by emptiness and a big gray rat Longhurst had taken to calling Fred.

"Tell you what, I'll shoot Fred and you can have the shed for free up until I vacate for Montana . . . if you don't mind rough shelter," he said.

"Best deal I expect to get," I replied.

"Better than Fred's part, at least. It'll be good to have you about, McCan. Fred makes for sorry company."

* * *

Over the next few days I kept thinking about Montana. Talking to Taylor again had awakened a pining in me for familiar places and faces. As rough as times had occasionally been for me up about Timber Creek, there had also been lots of good times. Going back might be pleasant . . . uncomfortable, too, but on the whole pleasant.

I decided to ask Longhurst about it as his final day as Cheyenne deputy approached. In the meantime, I had to find something to do with myself, so I went out looking for temporary work. All I could find was penny-ante duty as a dishwasher and stove-stoker at that same cafe where Longhurst and I had exchanged stories. It wasn't much of a job, but it put a little new money in my pocket and kept me off the streets . . . and out of the gambling houses.

One evening, as I left the restaurant, Longhurst came pounding up to me, out of breath and rather worked up. I was surprised, for he was normally the most easygoing of men.

"McCan, I hoped I'd catch you here. Come back with me to the jail. There's somebody there I want you to see."

"Why?"

"Because he won't give us his name, and I think you know him. He's a British-sounding gent who's jailed for trying to stab a fellow who was with him. The fellow got away—but they say he was a big one-eared Indian. Just like the one you described."

I raised my brows. "I'll be darned. Big Jim and Swallows-Beasley here in Cheyenne! Couldn't be any others."

"My thoughts exactly."

Sure enough, it was Swallows-Beasley in the cell. He looked mighty ragged around the edges, mostly because he was drunk. He looked at me but didn't seem to remember me. I suppose he thought I was just another deputy. Longhurst questioned him in my presence.

"Is your name Swallows-Beasley?" he asked him straight out.

Swallows-Beasley looked very surprised. "How did you—" He cut off, but it was too late. He had already confirmed the identification.

"Never mind how. This partner you had a row with, does he go by the name of Big Jim?"

Swallows-Beasley looked surprised again. He nodded compliantly, probably wondering if Longhurst was a mind reader.

"Well, Mr. Swallows-Beasley, I suggest you start opening your mouth and talking. I happen to know that a little English squirt and a big one-eared redskin are said to have led a mob that burned a mining town down west of Fort Collins not long ago. I expect the Colorado authorities would be very interested in getting their hands on either of those two."

Swallows-Beasley looked scared. A thin trail of drool escaped the corner of his mouth; he wiped it on the back of a shaky hand. You could smell the liquor on him from five feet away.

"What do you want to know?" he asked Longhurst.

"Why you tried to knife this Big Jim character, to start with."

"We argued," Swallows-Beasley replied. "We always argue a lot. This time it was worse than usual."

"What did you argue about?"

"About where to go. We had been down near Walden City, operating a saloon, you see. It was burned down—Big Jim was sure it was an old enemy of his who did it. A man named Smith, Fiddler Smith. He was the law in Walden City at the time the saloon burned. Big Jim got wind that Fiddler Smith had left Walden City with a woman. He got hot to follow them and even up his score with Smith. I went along with Big Jim—I've always tried to go along with him more than he had a right to expect, truth be told. We figured they would head this way. We sniffed around, asked questions, finally picked up their trail. It brought us to Cheyenne.

"By the time we got here, I was ready to forget about Fiddler Smith. I wanted to go to Nebraska. Big Jim wouldn't hear of it; he's got it inside his thick head again that Fiddler Smith has to die. Big Jim was acting just like he did the last time."

"The last time? What do you mean?" Longhurst asked.

"I mean the time once before that Big Jim was hot to kill Fiddler Smith. Over in Kansas. Big Jim stumbled across Fiddler Smith in a saloon; they went it at tooth and claw. Smith got away, though he did leave an ear behind."

"So *that*'s how he lost that ear," I commented. Swallows-Beasley glanced over at me and studied me. He was beginning to recognize me, I thought.

"So Big Jim and this Fiddler Smith are old enemies and from time to time get it in their heads to try to kill each other. Is that what you're saying?" Longhurst asked.

"That's the long and short of it, yes sir," Swallows-Beasley answered.

"Why do they hate each other?"

"Because of Craig City. The Independent Army of 1879. You know of that?"

"I do," Longhurst said. "How do Big Jim and Fiddler Smith fit in?"

"All I know is what Big Jim has told me. Those days were long before we took up together. Big Jim says that Fiddler Smith was in the Independent Army. He says Fiddler Smith killed his family and tried to kill him to turn in his ears for bounty. He didn't kill him, and he only managed to get one ear. Big Jim has hated him ever since."

"That's understandable," Longhurst said. "Now let's get back to the present situation. What happened after you and Big Jim tracked Fiddler and this female to Cheyenne?"

"We lost their trail. And that was fine with me; as I told you, I was ready to let Fiddler Smith go anyway. After a time, a man grows weary of chasing someone else's enemy. But Big Jim wouldn't let it go. He asked questions all around town, until at last he found a saloon-keeper who had been posting bills about a horse for sale. He finally sold the horse, he told Big Jim, to a one-eared man who was traveling with a woman, and needed a mount strong enough to carry the woman at least as far as Powderville, Montana."

"That's Fiddler, sure as the world," I said. "He was bound for Powderville after Walden City. He has a brother there."

Swallows-Beasley flashed me another suspicious look, but as of yet had not placed who I was.

"So what happened next?" Longhurst asked.

"Big Jim was ready to ride up to Powderville and try to catch Fiddler Smith. I told him no, I had already had my fill of tracking and chasing—I was ready to go to Nebraska and make some new money. Big Jim wouldn't listen; he was determined to head for Montana. We argued, I pulled out my knife, and lo and behold, here I am in your jail."

"And Big Jim?"

"Bound for Montana alone, and may he go to the devil, if the devil will have him."

Swallows-Beasley looked at me again. Recognition lit his eyes.

"*You!*" he declared.

"Yes indeed," I replied.

Swallows-Beasley waved toward me. "Deputy, this man is the very one who helped Fiddler Smith burn down my saloon! You must arrest him!"

"Out of my jurisdiction," Longhurst said. "Besides, you're going to be too busy explaining to the Colorado law why you burned Walden City to worry over one little saloon. Good day to you, Mr. Swallows-Beasley. God save the king."

We ate our suppers from cans that night, seated in Longhurst's little rented shack. I was about to bring up my wish to accompany him when he went to Montana, when he turned the situation around and brought it up first.

"McCan, I been thinking—you're at loose ends right now. Why not go with me up to Montana?"

I grinned. "I've been thinking along the same lines myself."

"Good to hear it. Bet there's a lot of folks you'd like to look up, huh?"

"There are. Likely as not I'll find some of them

moved off and others dead . . . but it hasn't been all that long. There's bound to be lots of familiar faces around the Timber Creek ranch.''

''And the Upchurch Emporium, too.'' He looked at me with a twinkle in his eye. Though Longhurst and I had first met only after Maggie had already married Rodney Upchurch—we met the very day of her wedding, in fact—he knew of my prior relationship with her.

''If you're talking about Maggie, I admit I'd like to see her. Not that it can do me any good with her still married to Upchurch.''

''Maybe she's not married anymore.''

''Why do you say that?''

''Didn't I tell you? A couple of months ago I got a letter from one of my old fellow Montana lawmen. Monroe Starr. Monroe is the kind to keep up with everybody's news. He was over about the Upchurch area, and everybody was talking about how Rodney Upchurch had taken bad sick in his lungs and was likely to pass on soon. You know how he'd been bedridden for a long time anyway.''

I did know. I remembered clearly the night that Evan Bridger shot Upchurch, prompting that final pursuit that ended in Bridger's death. Upchurch hadn't been expected to survive at all, but survive he had, though in a pitiable condition.

''So Maggie might already be a widow,'' I said, mostly to myself.

''That she might.''

I stood and walked over to the door. Opening it, I stared out toward the north. It made me feel ghoulish to take the report of Upchurch's likely death as good news—but I meant no harm by the feeling, and couldn't help how I felt anyway.

Maggie . . . free again, marriageable. What a thought!

Long ago I gave up any hope that she would ever be mine. When I met Cynthia, I put all thoughts of Maggie behind. But now Cynthia was dead. My circumstances were much changed, and maybe Maggie's, too.

"Yes sir, Longhurst," I said. "I do believe Montana is exactly where I need to go."

"Then, go you will. Of course, you got to consider one thing. There'll be more than just Maggie Upchurch up in Montana. There'll be Fiddler Smith and Big Jim, too."

"Maybe, if they make it that far before one finds and kills the other. And even if they do, what does it matter? Montana's a big place. I doubt I'll lay eyes again on either one of them."

PART TWO

BACK TO MONTANA

Chapter 13

It was good to travel with a friend again, good to be on the open trail, good to be riding toward the place where lived a lady I had loved and perhaps would love again. Twice in my life I had known what it was to love a fine woman and see that woman taken from me. Perhaps now it would be different. My dreams were big ones again.

The trail we followed northward was an old cattleman's-route. To the west rose the high Rockies, sun-glinting and magnificent; to the east lay the vast plains, stretching across Nebraska, Iowa, reaching over into Illinois. Days passed quickly, miles trailed off behind us. Now Cheyenne was distant, Walden City even more so. That unpleasant interlude in my life seemed dead and gone. A new time had come. Montana had until recently symbolized a finished interlude as well; now it symbolized the future. I hoped that there I would find the peaceful, settled life that had always eluded me.

From time to time I would think of Fiddler Smith and Vera Ann. Probably they had come this way—with Big Jim following. The more I thought about it, the more a sense of distress overtook my happiness. I had reason enough to be angry at Fiddler, given his abandonment of me the night he burned Big Jim's saloon. And, if Fiddler had in fact murdered Big Jim's family back in the Independent Army days, he was a more evil man than I would have ever thought. If Big Jim caught up with him, Fiddler would deserve any punishment that resulted.

Vera Ann Walden, however, was another story. She was no angel, as her illegitimate pregnancy sufficed to show, but beyond her promiscuity I knew of no fault in her. There was the distressing thing: If Big Jim caught up with Fiddler, he would also catch up with Vera Ann. And the odds were, she would fall victim to him right along with her unfortunately chosen partner.

I expressed this fear to Longhurst the day after we crossed the North Platte. He frowned, thoughtfully sniffed a pinch of snuff up his nose, and shook his head. "I got no answer for that one, McCan. It is a worrisome thought. But take heart—this here's a vast country. I'm betting that Big Jim will never find them."

"But he knows they're bound for Powderville," I replied. "If nothing else he'll probably find them there."

Longhurst shrugged. I could tell the thought of a pregnant woman being harmed, maybe killed, by a hardcase like Big Jim troubled him, but Longhurst tended not to worry long about what he couldn't control. I lacked that enviable trait; I tended to worry over everything. In silence I sent up a prayer for the safety of Vera Ann Walden, wondering if I would ever know its answer. It seemed unlikely that I would ever see that troubled woman again.

We crossed into the Montana country and headed toward Miles City. Some miles over the line, a couple of things happened that diverted our plans. First, Longhurst began to get sick. He had complained for the last two days of sore joints and a queasy stomach. Now he began vomiting everything he ate and drank, and he rode leaning over his saddle like a wounded man.

"You're in no shape to make Miles City," I said.

"I can make it," he answered. "Just keep riding."

So we rode, until the second obstacle met us the next morning, when Longhurst's horse threw a shoe after we crossed the Powder River.

"Got anything to fix it with?" I asked him.

"Nope. I appear to be a jinx, eh?"

I sighed. "Well, there's a town fifteen, twenty miles off. We'll just have to go there."

"What town is it?"

"You'd never guess."

He thought a moment, looked back at the river, then put on an expression of irony. "Powderville?"

"That's right."

He chuckled weakly. "Well, McCan, it looks like you might meet up with Fiddler Smith again after all."

"If he made it this far," I said. "Come on, let's go."

I let Longhurst ride my horse, since he was sick. As I led his limping mount, I wondered if in fact we would see Fiddler and Vera Ann in Powderville. Perhaps all this was intended to happen.

Maybe I would see them and be able to warn them about Big Jim—if he hadn't already caught up with them. After all, he left Cheyenne well before we did.

Longhurst was feeling much better by the time we reached Powderville. The sun had just edged down. The little settlement was well-lighted, a welcome sight for two weary travelers. I pointed out a little cafe that was sending out enticing smells of frying beef and baking biscuits.

Longhurst's appetite was back in a big way. We ordered a hearty meal and Longhurst ate like a starved refugee. I wasn't as hungry. Being in Powderville made me edgy; all I could think about was whether Fiddler and Vera Ann had made it here.

Across the dirt street a little saloon was doing middling business. I peered out the window, sipping my coffee as Longhurst put away a second round of biscuits and honey. Just as I drained off my last swallow, the wind shifted and carried noise from the saloon to my ears. I perked up when I heard the clear strains of fiddle music.

Longhurst heard it, too, and looked at me meaningfully. "You reckon?"

"It could be," I said, setting down the cup. "Guess I ought to go see, huh?"

"Guess so."

We paid, left, and walked across the street. The fiddle music was clearer now. So distinctive was its style that I knew even before entering the saloon that I had indeed found my old Walden City companion.

Fiddler stood in the corner, beside a broken-down piano, sawing the strings with vigor and sending up puffs of rosin dust that mixed with the smoke of his cigarette.

We went to the bar and ordered beers. Fiddler hadn't noticed me. I felt a strange impulse to leave before he saw me, but fought it down, feeling that perhaps this meeting was fated. The whole thing was peculiarly unsettling. There was comfort, at least, in knowing Fiddler was alive. Big Jim hadn't gotten him yet.

But what about Vera Ann? She was not here. I determined to find out about her, and so stood drinking my beer, staring straight at Fiddler and waiting for him to see me.

You've never heard as sour a fiddle drag as the one Fiddler Smith produced the moment his eyes met mine. Longhurst turned his head to hide his smile. It really was funny, as I think back on it, though at the time I didn't crack a smile. I kept my eyes focused straight on Fiddler's, taking a slow sip from my mug.

Somebody in the saloon gave a catcall. Fiddler ignored it and lowered his fiddle. He had stopped playing in midtune.

He glanced toward the door, licked his lips, then looked back at me. Resigning himself, he strode forward and joined me at the bar.

"Hello, McCan."

"Hello, Fiddler. I see you made it to Powderville."

"I made it."

"I'm glad. I was afraid something bad had happened to you. That happens sometimes, you know. A man can get hurt on the trail. Why, he might even get near-lynched by a mob that's mad because some fool burned down their watering hole."

Fiddler's face was as white as a sheet. "I owe you an apology, McCan. I shouldn't have hit you, and shouldn't have left you. I been worried about it ever since."

"Not worried enough to come back and check, I noticed."

He tried to swallow, but his throat must have been too dry. "I was drunk that night. I didn't know what I was doing. I was long gone from Walden City before it came to me that they might have found you lying out there."

"They found me. They came darn near to stringing me up. I'm lucky to be alive."

"I'm sorry. Really I am."

"Why didn't you come back, Fiddler? I thought you a better man than to run out on a friend. Or maybe I just thought I was your friend."

"Don't talk like that, McCan. You know I think the world of you. It was just the liquor, and being all crazy over Vera Ann. That's what did it."

"But you didn't come back. That's what galls me."

"I seen the smoke rising from the distance. I could see the light from the fire in the sky. I admit I was scared."

"They burned near the whole town, that mob. Burned it with Big Jim right at the head of it all. He was looking for you."

"Lord have mercy on me," Fiddler said. He leaned against the bar, laid down his fiddle and bow, and waved for a beer. As he drank it, his hands shook. Longhurst, seeing that this was not his affair, slipped off farther down the bar.

"Where's Vera Ann?" I asked

Fiddler looked pained. "Gone. She ran out on me."

"That right? How did it happen?"

"Out on the trail, it was. We were near the Black Hills. She told me the baby she's carrying wasn't mine, that she was already carrying it when she first met me."

"So I was right about her."

Fiddler grew angry at once. "Don't you talk bad about Vera Ann," he said. "I still care about that gal a mighty lot."

"Where is she now?"

"Still in the Black Hills. She said she had friends there, and made me take her over to Deadwood. I tried to talk her out of it. I told her I would marry her, raise that baby like my own." He shook his head and went red and moist in the eyes. "She wouldn't even listen to me. She shook me off like I was no more than a dog."

"So you came on to Powderville alone."

"Yeah."

"Did you find your brother?"

"I found him, all right. Found him in his grave." He wiped the back of his hand across his right eye. "He's been dead these three years, and I didn't even know it." He paused for a moment, looked away, then back at me again. "Why are you here, McCan? Did you come after me?"

"No. I'm heading up to Timber Creek and Upchurch. I've got some old friends to look up."

"Oh."

"Why'd you stay here, since your brother is dead?"

"A man has to stay somewhere. The fellow who runs the saloon gave me a fiddling job. Tips and free beer. Right now that's enough for me. There ain't nothing better worth doing out there, not with Vera Ann gone. I'm finding it hard to care much what happens to me now.''

I studied him silently. Though I was still mad as blazes at him, forgiveness was starting to slip in. Fiddler Smith seemed more worthy of pity than fury.

I gave a sigh of resignation. ''Well, I came out alive. You can rest your mind about that. Ike Walden wasn't as lucky.''

''What happened to Walden?''

''He's dead. Killed by that mob you stirred up. They blamed him for ordering the saloon burned. But it wasn't his fault, was it? It was you doing that on your own, trying to hurt Big Jim. Right?''

He lowered his head, ''Right.''

''You'd have been better off just to have shot that Indian instead of torching his building. He got out just fine, and now he's after you.''

''After me?''

''He found out where you were heading, and came after you. You owe some thanks to Vera Ann, Fiddler. She probably saved your life, diverting you off to the Black Hills when she did. I'm betting that Big Jim passed you by while you were there.''

Fiddler really looked scared now. He turned up his beer and didn't stop gulping until it was gone.

''Big Jim's after me?'' He said it as if trying to comprehend it. ''He was that set on finding me?''

''So I hear. That's what his partner told me when I saw him in a jail cell in Cheyenne.'' I took a softer tone. ''You got to consider he may still be looking for you, Fiddler. Watch out for him. If he finds you, he'll kill you.''

Fiddler nodded. He wore a blank, scared stare. "I thank you for the warning, McCan. God above, I'm sorry I done you like I did. Maybe I would have come back if I hadn't had Vera Ann to watch out for. Yeah, I would have come back—it's Vera Ann I was worried about."

Maybe it was true, or maybe it was just Fiddler looking for some way to justify to himself the wrong he had done me. It didn't matter now.

"Well, Fiddler, all's said that needs saying, as far as I'm concerned. Most likely our paths won't cross again. I forgive you for what you did." It took all my will to do it, but I stuck out my hand. "You watch out for yourself, hear? And keep a lookout for Big Jim."

"I will," he said. His handshake was trembly. "Bless your soul, Luke McCan. You're a better man than I'll ever be."

"There's none of us good men when it comes down to it, Fiddler. We're all just blind folks stumbling along as best we can."

When Longhurst and I left, Fiddler was drinking another beer. I gave him a long look from the door, figuring it to be the last time I would see him, then exited into the night.

Chapter 14

It's hard to describe my feelings when we rode into Miles City. My thoughts had lately been turned toward the future, but seeing this town again pulled me back into the past. Things had changed—the town was bigger, and somehow brighter—yet so much was the same. On main street stood the livery with its bow-shaped sign, the familiar blacksmith shop, the bakery, the Chinese laundry butted up against the meat market. My feelings ran counter to each other: I was home again, yet also a newcomer in a strange land.

Even in the bright sunlight I could feel ghosts of my past hovering all around me. Or maybe I was the ghost, visiting again the places I had haunted in life.

I looked for Maggie as I rode, though I had no reason to expect her to be in town. A question burned in my mind: Was Rodney Upchurch still alive?

Longhurst was in high spirits. He grinned at all we passed, and tipped his hat to the women. We were gritty and bearded from our long ride, so we found a hotel and checked ourselves in after stabling our horses at the livery. A barber's parlor next door offered baths, and we took advantage. The soapy water washed the dirt from our bodies and eased the aches of days in the saddle. So far, no one I had seen had given any indication of recognizing me.

I made conversation with the barber and found the answer I had been seeking.

"Rodney Upchurch? Oh, yeah—sad situation. The poor fellow passed away three weeks ago. I didn't know him, but they say he was a good man. I did know his father; he operated a big store right here in town for years."

Confirmation of Upchurch's death intensified my contradictory feelings. On the one hand it made me feel sad for Maggie, who surely was in grief. On the other hand, there's no denying that having my old rival out of the picture did open new opportunities for me.

"Who's running the big Upchurch store?" I asked.

"Maggie Upchurch, all alone. Quite a determined woman, that one. Pretty, too."

"Amen to that," I said beneath my breath. The barber heard me.

"You know Maggie Upchurch? I assumed you were a newcomer, sir."

"I am, in a way. But I lived here for a time, working for the Timber Creek Cattle Enterprise."

"You don't say? Well then, welcome back, Mr . . ."

"McCan. Luke McCan."

"I'll bet you've got lots of old friends to look up."

"I do—but don't spread word about me yet. I want to surprise people, you know."

Afterward, Longhurst said, "I thought you were in a big rush to find all your old buddies."

"I thought I was. Now that I'm here, it feels different. I want to settle in slow, not hurry anything."

"Maggie Upchurch in particular?"

"Yeah." I grinned self-consciously. "I guess I'm a little nervous about how she's going to react to seeing me. I might be the last person she wants to lay eyes on."

"Don't wait too long," Longhurst said. "She's a very marriageable woman right now. Somebody could steal her out from under your nose again. Heck, I might just do it myself!"

"You do, and I'll skin you. Stick to flirting with your saloon girls and leave Maggie to me."

Longhurst dug out his snuffbox. "Come on," he said. "We've got land and cattle to buy. Taylor Longhurst is ready to start ranching."

"Don't get yourself too worked up, Longhurst," I said. "It can take a long time to build up a cattle business."

My prediction, to Longhurst's delight, held about as much water as a bottomless bucket. Within three days he had scouted down a disgruntled small-time cattleman itchy to rid himself of both land and herd. He had suffered several strokes of bad fortune and felt pressed to return to Illinois to take care of ailing parents. Exactly one week after our arrival, Longhurst was passing money and signing papers in a lawyer's office—some of the money being mine, for I had decided to buy into the operation—

and we walked out onto Main Street as owners of what Longhurst dubbed the L&M Cattle Company.

It felt good to be part of the landed class. Of course, true to my nature, I had a thousand worries rolling around in my mind. I had gone at once from being a responsibility-free drifter to facing duties and risks. Longhurst and I would have to worry about weather, disease, rustlers, all the common threats facing cattlemen. And there were only the two of us to run the ranch, with little cash remaining to hire help. It would take time before we began making money. Within an hour of closing our transaction, I had already mentally mapped out a dozen potential roads to poverty, any one of which we might find ourselves on.

Longhurst, as usual, seemed to have no such worries. He knew less about the cattle business than I did, and felt sure that nothing but wealth lay ahead of us. As for our meager remaining cash, he was ready to spend a chunk of it on celebrating the founding of our enterprise.

I couldn't deny Longhurst that celebration, my thought being that we probably wouldn't be able to afford such frivolities for a long time afterward. That night we toured the Miles City saloons and dance halls. I was pleasantly surprised to find myself repelled rather than attracted by the gambling tables. Maybe this ranching investment was just what I had needed to steer me into a more stable course of life.

I met a couple of old acquaintances in one of the saloons. Neither was a close friend, but both found it big news that Luke McCan was back in the area and going into business. It would not take long now for word of my return to spread. Soon

Maggie would know I was back. I wondered how that would make her feel—if it would make her feel anything at all.

"It seems a prime time for you to go look Maggie up," Longhurst suggested. "Now you're a respectable man of business. She'll be impressed."

"I'll look her up soon," I said. "All in good time."

Two weeks went by and the good time never came. Partly it was because Longhurst and I were extremely busy, taking stock of the herd, repairing the dismal log ranch house that was now our home, and doing all the hundred other things required to revive a lagging ranch operation.

Our ranch house stood about midway between Rosebud and Miles City. The previous owner had let it, and the operation in general, run down considerably. The roof leaked, the walls were poorly chinked, and the dirt floor was uneven. By merit of my superior carpentry skills—and Longhurst's superior excuse-making—most of the repair work fell to me.

This kept me away from much human contact for many days. Though I griped enough about it to keep up a good front for Longhurst, I really didn't mind the isolation. For reasons I couldn't explain, I didn't feel the need for company. Some of it might have stemmed from my troubled times in Walden City. Some of it might have been because I still wasn't sure that I was ready to see Maggie. I was like the little storybook boy in London who longed to meet Father Christmas, then lagged back and hid his head in his mother's skirts when at last he met a man costumed as the character at a children's party.

As long as my reunion with Maggie was a dream, a thing as of yet not real, I could imagine it falling out the way I longed for it to. The real thing, in which Maggie's reaction would be controlled by herself, not my wishes, might be a far different affair.

My isolation was soon to end. Old friends, having heard I was in the area, began riding out to see me. Even bearish old Stewart Biggs, a veteran cowpoke who had tried to get my dander up when I was a greenhorn back at Timber Creek years ago, rode out to say hello and fill me in on news of the ranch. I could tell he wasn't happy there anymore; things had changed since the old days.

"Ever since we lost Dan Tackett and Abe Hunt, it's been a dee-cline, a steady dee-cline." That's the way he said it. "That little Iowa worm Henry Sandy is still there, running the place. He's losing money, so likely he'll be gone soon enough. Of course, I been telling myself that for the last two years, and he ain't gone yet." Biggs fidgeted. "I might just up and leave . . . if I had another good spread to go to work for."

None too subtle was Stewart Biggs. Unfortunately, I couldn't give him the answer he was fishing for. "Stewart, if I can ever roust enough work out of Longhurst to make a go of this place, I expect we'll have need of some good men. Right now, though, it's slim pickin's for hired work at the L&M."

He looked disappointed. "Well, then, I might come checking later—if you don't mind it."

"I'd be offended if you didn't. Thanks for coming to see me."

Biggs bowlegged it over to his waiting horse and

mounted with a loud wheeze of exertion. He was aging now; it made me sad.

"Oh!" he said. "I plumb forgot. Maggie Upchurch said to tell you hello. I was out by the Empórium before I come out here, and she sent the word."

I wondered if Biggs could see my shirt jumping from the pounding of my heart. "Tell her hello, too. How's she doing, now that her husband's gone?"

"Truth is, I think she's doing better than when he was living, even though it sounds a bad thing to say. She had to tend to him like he was a baby at the end. Now that he's gone, she can have some peace."

"I hope so." Biggs turned and began to ride away. I called to him and he wheeled again.

"Tell Maggie I'll be up her way in a day or two. I'll stop in the Emporium. I'd like to say hello."

Biggs touched his hat and nodded, then rode off. I watched his horse kicking up dust until it was far away. Entering the house, I looked myself over in the broken glass that served as our mirror. Unshaven, dirty, unshorn . . . I looked like I had just come off a long winter's line camp.

That night, over eggs and beef, I told Longhurst I'd not be working about the ranch the next day. I had things to do in Miles City.

"Like what?" He sounded grumpy; he knew that me away from the ranch would mean more work for him.

"Like getting a shave and a bath and some new clothes."

His brows went up. "Going up to Upchurch at last, I take it?"

"You got it right. I want to see that lady again. I've been too long a-waiting already."

Longhurst poked his fork at me. "Don't you up and get married on me and leave me to run this ranch alone."

"Run it? Run it broke, you mean."

"I think I'm doing a fair job so far!"

I grinned at him. "Reckon you are. Think you can handle it for a day without me?"

"Think you're pretty all-fired important, don't you! Of course I can handle it. But I mean it: Don't you go getting yourself married. Don't you do it. Hear?"

"I hear."

Chapter 15

In my time I've faced gunmen and rustlers, outlaws and lawmen. None of them ever put my nerves on edge nearly as much as the sight of the Upchurch Emporium when I rode over the slope and saw it gleaming in the sun on the flat below. The big white building hadn't changed a bit since last I saw it, except that what appeared to be a new storage room had been added on the west side, and the place was now surrounded by several more houses, stables, and such. There was no denying that the little Upchurch community had become a true town.

The house Rodney Upchurch had built for himself and the bride he had snatched from me was painted a clean light brown now, and looked smaller for it. There was Maggie's flower garden, still brown and winter-dried; there were her carefully nurtured young fruit trees. Across the backyard stretched a clothesline, some of Maggie's dresses flapping on it in the cool wind. Even from this distance I recognized two as dresses Maggie had worn during our courting days. I had to smile. Despite the success of the Upchurch Emporium,

Maggie remained a true daughter of the frontier: unwasteful, unprideful, frugal. She would wear a dress until it was threadbare, then rip it into rag strips and use them to make rugs. There was no room for waste in plains life.

Nudging spurs against horseflesh, I began my long, circling descent to the Emporium, feeling so nervous I had to laugh at myself. All I was doing, after all, was saying hello to an old friend. I wasn't riding down to propose marriage.

Who was I fooling? The possibility of eventual marriage was at the very heart of all I was doing. This first reunion with Maggie could prove a door to a bright future. That door had been closed in my face when Maggie married Rodney Upchurch and then again when Cynthia died. This time, heaven willing, it would open. The choice would be Maggie's.

An expensive carriage shiny with varnish and polish sat in front of the Emporium. I tied my mount to the hitchpost and looked the rig over in admiration. Maggie's store was drawing some big-money customers these days.

At the door I took a deep breath and forced myself to walk straight in. And there she was: Maggie, as pretty as ever.

She didn't notice me, for she was embroiled in seemingly intense conversation with two well-dressed men. These fellows had big-city money written all over them; they surely accounted for that fine rig outside. From their bearing and manner, it was clear that theirs was a business visit. Slipping over behind a display of fabric rolls, I remained hidden from Maggie's view, not wanting to unnerve her by a sudden appearance in the midst of what looked to be an important conversation.

I wasn't trying to listen to the talk, but the taller of the two men had one of those voices that crawls through the air and reaches every corner of a room even when softly spoken. I detected very quickly that these men were proposing to buy out the store.

"Mrs. Upchurch, I hope you'll reconsider," the tall one said. "A young widow such as yourself needs to be free of burdening duties such as this store imposes." The man's voice, though still low, had a quality that told me he and Maggie were in tense disagreement.

"Mr. Bell, I've been accustomed not only to operating this store, but doing so with an invalid husband who required nearly constant attention. Now that he's passed on, God rest him, the burden of my duties is lighter, not heavier. This store is my livelihood and I have no desire to sell it."

A short pause. "Mrs. Upchurch, I want this store. I've made you a good offer and I cannot understand why you won't take it!"

"I've explained myself clearly, I think."

Another pause—then I almost jumped out of my boots when the lanky Mr. Bell pounded the nearby countertop so hard that it rattled the candy jars on the far end. I came around from behind the on-end fabric rolls and saw Maggie stepping back, a look of alarm on her face. Bell swore in a most ungentlemanly manner.

Seeing him talk so to Maggie flew all over me. I strode forward.

"I think you'd best leave, friend," I said.

Three faces turned to me, all bearing expressions of surprise—Maggie's most of all. Bell lifted his hands and turned again to Maggie, keeping me in the corner of his eye. "Look, Mrs. Upchurch, I apologize. I'm a man of hot temper and it got the best of me."

"That's a good apology," I said. "Fine job. Now get on out of here."

Bell's partner stepped forward and said, "Now, listen here . . ." Bell put a hand on his shoulder and stopped him. Together they walked out. Bell was about to slam the door, but thought better of it and caught it before it hit. He eased it shut. A few moments later the fancy buggy clattered away.

"Hello, Maggie," I said, smiling at her.

She looked at me like I was foulness on legs, "Luke McCan, how dare you walk in here out of the blue and interfere with my business? Who do you think you are, anyway? My champion? I'm perfectly capable of dealing with my own affairs myself, Mr. McCan!"

She spun on her heel and stomped back to the little office at the back of the store, entered, and pounded the door shut. I was left speechless, alone in the midst of the big store.

A moment later anger came. I wheeled, and stomped back to the entrance. I wasn't as restrained as the last man to exit this door: I slammed it as hard as I could, hard enough to make sure Maggie Carrington Upchurch heard it back in her office.

She didn't seem surprised to see me when she emerged from the store that evening. I was leaning against a tree, smoking and waiting for her, for my anger had cooled—as I hoped hers had as well. She smiled and slowly shook her head as she approached. Time hadn't changed her at all; there wasn't another day of age in that perfect oval face, still girlishly freckled. Her dark hair did not frame her face as I remembered it. She wore it pulled up and tied with a plain ribbon—a merchantess's concession to practicality, yet it did not diminish her attractiveness one bit.

"Luke," she said, drawing near and extending her hand. "It's good to see you again."

I took her hand in both of mine—it was marvelous to touch her again after all this time—and gently squeezed it. "It's good to see you, too, Maggie. Reckon I picked just the wrong way to say my hello earlier today."

She smiled a healing smile. "I was on edge—it was me who was wrong, not you. I know you were just trying to help. That Bell man has been after me to sell out to him since just after Rodney's burial. Maybe now he'll leave me alone at last."

"Well, if he doesn't, you just let me know and . . ." I stopped. "Doing it again, aren't I? I can't seem to get it through my head that you're able to take care of yourself."

"I have no choice."

"I heard about that. You've got my condolences, Maggie. I know it's a hard thing to lose someone you love."

We walked together and talked for the next hour. She told me of the difficult long months of Upchurch's alternating improvements and declines; I told her about my time in Missouri and the loss of Cynthia. Strange, how easy it was to talk to her about Cynthia.

She was fascinated with the story of Walden City and Fiddler Smith, though the latter portions horrified her. "You might have been killed,

Luke!'' she said—and she said it like it was an important matter to her.

"I might have been, but I wasn't. I'm mighty glad, too. I would have missed the chance to see you again."

"I'm glad you came, Luke. And I wish you and Mr. Longhurst the best of luck on your new ranch."

"Thank you, Maggie." We stood silently, looking at each other until it felt uncomfortable. "Maggie . . . you mind if I come back sometime to see you again?"

"I hope you will."

"Good. Good. I'll be back, then. Well . . . good-bye for now."

"Good-bye, Luke."

I sang all the way back to the ranch.

Two days later I was in Miles City buying nails and groceries, when I looked across the street and saw a sight that made me drop my bundles on the boardwalk. A woman was walking there, carrying a bag and looking as sad as she was pregnant. It was none other than Vera Ann Walden.

I found nothing pleasant in seeing her. Every bad memory from Walden City flooded back, along with new concerns. Why was she here? Fiddler had said she had intended to remain in the Black Hills with friends.

It would have been easy to let her walk on past, to ride back to the ranch, and forget about her. Yet I couldn't do that . . . especially not with her looking as forlorn as she did. If ever I had seen a woman in need of help, it was Vera Ann at that moment.

So I laid my bundles in the wagon, walked out onto the street, and called to her. She turned, surprised to hear her name called, and watched me cross to meet her. Surely she was as taken aback by the sight of me as I was in seeing her.

"Luke!" Her voice sounded weak and shaky.

"Vera Ann, I'm surprised to see you here. I thought you were in Black Hills."

"I was, then I had to—But how do you know about where I was? Nobody here . . . knows . . . oh, I'm so weak . . ."

"Vera Ann!"

I caught her as she started to fall. Her face was as white as milk. It made for quite a scene, me grasping at a fainting pregnant woman right on the sunny central street of Miles City. Several people came running up, alarmed. Is she all right? What's happened? Did you hurt her?

What had happened was that Vera Ann had fainted from hunger. I fanned her awake right there on the boardwalk and she admitted that she had not eaten a bite for two days.

"Well, you'll eat today," I said. "Come on— let's get you over to the cafe and put some victuals down you."

Despite her obvious hunger, Vera Ann ate slowly. Her hand shook every time she lifted her fork. Here was a woman who had been through hard times.

"Where did you see Fiddler?" she asked me, a desperate edge on the query.

"In Powderville. It wasn't a planned meeting, but I'm glad it happened. I was able to warn him that he was in danger."

"Danger? What kind of danger?"

"There's a big Sioux Indian after him . . . at least, there was. I don't know the situation now. It's an old enemy of Fiddler's, not to mention being one of the owners of the saloon Fiddler burned down outside Walden City."

"Burned? What are you talking about?"

I was amazed. Vera Ann didn't even know what had happened outside Walden City that night—either that, or she was putting on one convincing act.

I realized abruptly that there was one detail she could not know, and needed to: the death of her father. My strength drained away; I sank back in my chair, dreading what I had to reveal.

"Vera Ann," I said gently, "there are some things you must know about. One thing in particular I have to tell you, and it's not easy: Your father is gone. He was killed the night you left Walden City."

Vera Ann's eyes went red and moist. A tear trailed down her cheek and she lowered her head, saying not a word.

"I'll start at the beginning and tell it straight through," I said. "That's the easiest way to make sense of it all."

I laid out the story: the torching of the saloon, my abandonment by Fiddler, the destruction of Walden City by Big Jim's mob, and the defiant death of Ike Walden. She stared at her plate as I told it, asking no questions, making no comments.

"Now I want to hear what's happened to you since I saw you last," I said to her. "Why are you in Miles City?"

She spoke in a quiet, slightly trembling voice. Some of what she said I already knew. She had become pregnant sometime before Fiddler Smith and I had arrived in Walden City. Knowing her stern father would deal with her harshly over the pregnancy, she tried to lure either Fiddler or me to take her away before the truth was known. Fiddler had taken the bait, and she had sunk her hook deeper into him by telling him, falsely, that the child she carried was his.

Once far away from Walden City, however, the guilt of that lie had weighed on her, combined with a growing sense of doubt about whether she really wanted to spend her life with Fiddler Smith as her mate. She confessed to him the truth about her pregnancy, then made up the story about friends in the Black Hills as a way of getting him to set her free. He did so, however reluctantly, and took Vera Ann to Deadwood.

Life as a lone, unmarried, pregnant woman in a little western Gomorrah like Deadwood had proven far more hellish than anything Vera Ann could have imagined. She started out with a fair stash of the money she and Fiddler had taken from Ike Walden the night of their flight, but it didn't last long. What wasn't spent was stolen, and before long Vera Ann found herself with only three options: starvation, prostitution, or finding Fiddler Smith again.

The last option had been the most appealing. With charm and the last of her cash, she convinced a wagoner to take her from Deadwood to Powderville, where she hoped to find Fiddler still visiting his much-talked-about brother. But the brother was dead and Fiddler wasn't there. He had been there, folks told her, but he had left abruptly after talking to a couple of drifters who showed up to get some farrier work done.

With tearful pleading Vera Ann had convinced the wagoner to take her on one final ride, this time up to Miles City. There, she hoped, she would find Fiddler, or at least some other person who would help her out. She had never dreamed, she said, that that person would be me. She had never expected to meet Luke McCan again.

I reached across the table and patted her hand. "I'm glad I found you," I said. "No woman should have to go through what you have, especially while she's carrying a child."

"What can I do, Luke?" she asked. "I still have no place to stay." Her eyes became soft and sincerely pleading—no deception, no conniving this time. "Can I stay at your ranch? At least for a while?"

"That wouldn't do, Vera Ann. People talk, you know. But there's a place I can take you, a lady I know who I feel sure will be glad to take you in and give you all the help she can. She's a good woman, a friend of mine, and her name is Maggie Upchurch."

Chapter 16

She was just as kind and generous about it as I could have ever hoped," I was telling Longhurst. "Maggie took Vera Ann in without a moment's hesitation, and before I left she was talking about new clothes and fixing up one of the extra rooms and getting a crib for when the baby comes." I nodded my head admiringly. "Maggie's quite a woman, Longhurst. Quite a woman. Everybody talking about how fine she is, taking in a 'soiled girl' like Vera Ann. That's how I heard somebody putting it."

Longhurst took a snort of snuff, sneezed, and said, "Vera Ann must think she's died and gone to heaven."

"It'd take a lot less than heaven to make her happy, with all she's been through," I said. "You know, it's nigh as much her fault as Fiddler's, all the trouble that happened at Walden City, but I can't seem to hold my anger at her over it. I just feel sorry for her, mostly."

Longhurst aimed a finger at me. "That's your very problem, McCan! Always pitying folks too much and getting messed up in their problems.

You'd get by better if you'd learn to mind your own business and stay out of everybody else's."

Before the next week was out, Longhurst had proven himself unable to live up to his own standards—and in the process gave me one more occasion to marvel at how things that you think are over and done with can rise up again before your eyes. Running into Fiddler at Powderville and encountering Vera Ann in Miles City had already stripped away my assurance that the Walden City affair was behind me.

On the following Tuesday morning, Longhurst rode into Miles City to talk to another cattleman about a possible small-scale land lease. I spent my day on the range with the herd; that evening I came loping slowly in, thinking about Maggie and feeling good about the world. The sun was setting and my stomach was grumbling for a feeding of beef and biscuits, our most usual nightly menu.

I dismounted and led my horse around to the little barn to feed it grain. Stretching to relieve saddle cramp, I fished out my fixings and began rolling a smoke. It was one of those rare moments when life is moving at the most perfect, lazy speed, pressures and worries a long way off.

I lit the cigarette and looked up through the smoke to see Longhurst barreling in at top speed. His horse was lathered and panting. The evening light was casting a strange shadow across the left side of Longhurst's face—then I saw it wasn't a shadow, but a fresh bruise.

"What the devil . . ."

"McCan, I'm glad I found you. There's trouble." Longhurst swung down off his perch and ran the horse into the corral without unsaddling it.

"So I see—and from that shiner, I'd say you found your way into the middle of it."

"This is serious business, McCan. It's Fiddler Smith."

"What?"

"You heard me—Fiddler. He's in Miles City, or was until he ran out. It's a good thing for him he ran, too, for he came nigh to getting himself killed."

"You sure it was Fiddler?"

" 'Course I'm sure. I seen him with my own eyes, didn't I?"

Blast it all. I had hoped Fiddler Smith wouldn't come crawling back through my life again. Why would he be in Miles City? I had a suspicion that whatever his reason, it had to do with Vera Ann.

"So what happened?"

"Well, I'd gone into a saloon to wash the dust out of my throat about the shank of the afternoon, when out across the street I heard a ruckus. I downed my beer and went out to see about it— reckon I can't get the lawman out of my blood— and what did I see but Fiddler Smith with a knife out, swinging it at a couple of big gents who were yelling and cussing at him."

"I didn't know what it was about or who was in the right or wrong, but I couldn't just stand there. I took off and started out to help Fiddler, when he spins, slashes one of the others across the upper arm, then kicks up like a saloon dancer and boots me right in the eye. That's right—boot! Them lanky legs have a right wide stretch, I'm here to tell you. I suppose he thought I was coming to hurt him instead of help.

"I went down like a feed sack, and Fiddler

jumped right over me and headed for his horse. He rode out before anybody could stop him.''

''Them two he had been fighting with came over and asked me if I was all right—I guess they figured, just like Fiddler, that I had been going to take their side in the fight. I asked them what it was about, and they said this one-eared gent had come into a saloon all drunk and rowdy, demanding to know where he could find his woman and Luke McCan. He said her name was Vera Ann Walden and he'd heard saloon gossip up around Glendive about Luke McCan taking in some pregnant female. I reckon he figured out it was Vera Ann.''

''The story I get is that Fiddler's hot to take up with Vera Ann again. How he feels about your part of things I don't know. I'm thinking he may believe you've stole his woman, and may try to hurt you for it.''

''Fiddler Smith's a fool,'' I said. ''I wish he'd ride off as far away from here as he could go. Well, go on, Longhurst. Did the law go after him?''

Longhurst's face was lighted orange by the setting sun; his expression became even more intense. ''Now, there's the most loco part of all, and let me tell you, it sends a chill right up my backbone! A deputy came sauntering over shortly after Fiddler rode off, and found out what had happened. I asked him if he was going to go after Fiddler and he said no, he didn't think he would. All he'd likely do if he caught Fiddler would be run him out of town, and he'd already gone off on his own, so there would be no point to that. But here's the thing that perked my attention: This deputy, as he's turning around, says; 'I've already had my fill of fooling with one-eared troublemakers today, anyhow.'

"First thing I thought of when he said that was this Big Jim character. I was putting two and two together, you see: if Fiddler Smith was about Miles City, then maybe Big Jim was, too. Maybe he'd still been looking for him and had followed him, you know. Sure enough, when I asked the deputy about it, he says this other one-eared man was a big ugly Indian, and he'd been going about town, scaring folks and asking real loud about a man named Smith, who he'd followed in from Glendive."

"Lord have mercy, Longhurst! You think Fiddler knows Big Jim is this close to him?"

"That I can't tell you. But I sure knew you'd want to know about this, in case Fiddler shows up gunning for you. Hell, he could lead Big Jim right here!"

"Or worse, he could find out where Vera Ann is and lead him up to Maggie's. Longhurst, do you know where Fiddler headed after he rode out of town?"

"No . . . but I can tell you that on the way here, I saw a durn big campfire burning along that little crick a couple of miles back."

My mind flashed back to that first night when Fiddler and I had shared camp, and how he had commented about never being able to abide a camp without a roaring fire. "It might be him—I'll go and see."

"You think that's smart, McCan? He might have designs to harm you, thinking you took Vera Ann and all."

"So he might—which means I'd rather find him than let him find me. Besides, whatever he may think about me, I want to warn him about Big Jim.

I won't do to him what he did to me when he left me for that mob to eat alive. Lord knows I hope I'm a better man than that."

"You're too good a man—so good you'll get yourself killed one of these days. But if you're set on going, let me get a fresh mount and go with you."

"Get the fresh mount, all right, but don't go with me. You've got to head up to Upchurch, fast as you can, and see to Maggie and Vera Ann until I can get there myself. I don't want Fiddler showing up there with them alone in that house and luring Big Jim to them."

Even stubborn old Longhurst saw the sense in that and did not argue. We worked quickly, preparing for our divergent rides. What had happened to that lazy evening I had been enjoying? It had vanished. The night now was heavy with threat and cooled by an urgent wind that said hurry, hurry, get going before the trouble that always follows Fiddler Smith catches up with you . . . or with Maggie.

The night was cool against my face as I rode toward the wooded creek, praying it in fact was Fiddler's camp Longhurst had seen . . . and praying that if it was Fiddler's, I would reach him before Big Jim did.

The fire was somewhat burned down by the time I drew in sight of the camp; still, its flames danced hot in the night breeze. I looked for the silhouette of a human form about the blaze and saw nothing. Dismounting, I unbooted my Winchester and crept forward, wondering if I should hail the camp and risk Fiddler shooting me in anger, or come in secretly. Either way had its dangers.

I chose the latter option, partly because the closer I drew, the more unsettled and uncertain I felt. Something was wrong here. The atmosphere didn't feel quite right. Trouble was about—or maybe already had come and gone.

Don't let me find him dead, I silently prayed. Don't let Big Jim have already gotten to him.

Why did I care? I didn't know. Fiddler Smith was no true friend of mine . . . but I did care. I didn't want to see a man I had ridden and worked with murdered by the same big savage that had almost taken my own life.

There, by the fire . . . a dark heap. Maybe a bedroll. Maybe a body.

Heart driving in my chest, I advanced. The wind moved the fire, sent sparks flying, made the circle of light dance and play over the mysterious heap that held my attention. It did look like a man now, a man in his blankets. Maybe he was sleeping—but if he was, why was there no motion of breath?

"Fiddler?" I said softly. "Fiddler, is that you?"

I kicked the blankets. Empty. Before I heard any sound, I knew I wasn't alone. Someone was behind me, and close. I spun on my heel and caught the flashing vision of a face not a yard from mine. Something swept down and struck the side of my head; I collapsed.

In that brief moment that I had seen the face, I knew what a terrible error I had made in coming into this camp. The face had been that of a big man, scarred and dark and missing an ear. The face of Big Jim.

Chapter 17

The next thing I was aware of was lying on my back, arms and legs outstretched. When I tried to move, I couldn't. My wrists and ankles felt like they were held in too-tight vises. Twisting my head, I saw that I was tied to four stout pegs driven into the earth. My head pounded in rhythm with the flickering of the big fire. So close was I to the blaze that sweat rolled off me; I was nearly being roasted alive.

Big Jim appeared above me, grinning down like a devil in a child's nightmare. He knelt, his swarthy face coming so near mine I could taste the foul breath blowing across his yellowed teeth.

"Looks like I caught me one of 'em, anyway," he said. "You're McCan."

"Let me go, Big Jim," I said in a gravelly voice. "You have no cause to hold me like this."

"Like hell!" he declared. "You got away from me once. Now you won't get away."

"What are you going to do to me?"

"Maybe nothing. Maybe you'll talk and tell Big Jim what he needs to know and I'll let you go."

That seemed unlikely; Big Jim didn't look the

sort to have an ounce of mercy in him. I felt like a fool, blundering into his camp as I had. In my zeal to find Fiddler, I had overlooked the possibility that my search would yield up the wrong man.

He leaned even closer. Firelight glittered on the ugly scar-nub where his ear had been, and on the ragged thing that once had been a nose. "You tell me where I can find Fiddler Smith and maybe I'll turn you loose."

"I don't know where he is."

"You know—you're his partner!"

"Not anymore. I haven't been his partner since Walden City."

He hit me so hard I fainted. When I came around again, he was kneeling on the other side of me, placing a flat stone beneath my bound left hand.

"What are you doing?"

"Nothing, if you talk."

"I told you—I don't know where Fiddler is!"

He lifted another stone, one almost as big as my head. "See if this helps you remember," he said. Then he brought down the stone.

I felt pain like I had never known, heard a mashing, snapping sound as he crushed my hand. I sent up a scream and almost passed out again.

"The next one will hurt even more," he said. "You talk to Big Jim now."

"I don't know . . . where he is . . ."

The stone came down again, and I did pass out. When I awakened, my hand had no feeling at all, and in a burst of panic I wondered if he had cut it off. Twisting my head, I was first relieved, then horrified. My hand was still there, but it was a pulpy, shattered thing, broken and bleeding. The numbness went away when I saw what he had done to me, and great throbs of pain rolled up my left arm.

"Where's Fiddler Smith?" Big Jim asked again.

"I swear to God above . . . I don't know."

"You like to hurt, McCan? I hope you do, because I haven't even started to make you hurt yet."

I closed my eyes and saw faces before me—people I had known and loved. Old friends from long past like Bill and Bob Webster, Caleb and Jerusha Black, Dan Tackett and Abe Hunt; my sister Martha . . . and my lost Cynthia. Then Maggie . . . and with her image came a burst of will. I had to get through this alive, to make sure that Big Jim never did to Maggie the sorts of things he was doing to me. I wished I had never taken Vera Ann to Maggie, for Vera Ann would draw Fiddler to where she was, and where Fiddler went, Big Jim would follow.

He was at my feet now, pulling off my right boot. I struggled and prayed toward the dark sky, asking for rescue, for whatever mercy God could grant a man who usually ignored him. I would have prayed for death, but death would wipe out any chance I might ever have to see to Maggie's safety. Maggie . . . I forced my mind to concentrate on her image. For Maggie I would have to endure Big Jim's tortures, and somehow come through alive.

I lifted my head and saw him at the fire, raising a burning brand. He was going to put fire to my bare foot. I tried to close my eyes and shut out the sight, but my eyes wouldn't obey me. I watched in terror as he began to kneel, a broad grin on his face.

I bit my lip, determined not to scream again, no matter what he did. And I didn't scream. I laughed

instead, for from the brush beside the camp clearing, suddenly came a figure that I was certain was
a guardian angel, sent in answer to my prayer . . .
except it struck me as peculiar that this guardian
angel carried a rifle, wore dirty clothing and a battered derby, and looked for all the world like Fiddler Smith. Apparently I fainted again, for all I can
recall from the next moments is the sound of a shot,
the noise of grappling, the shouting of most un-
angelic curses, then a second shot.

The face above me now was not ugly, like Big
Jim's, but beautiful. Lean, whiskered, homely,
single-eared—but beautiful beyond any face I had
ever seen. Cold steel touched my right wrist and I
felt my bonds being cut. He moved down to my
feet and freed them, then to my shattered left hand.
I heard him exclaim in horror at the sight of it;
when he cut the bonds on that side, I felt a new
wave of pain and almost fainted again.

"You're all right now, McCan," Fiddler
Smith's voice said. "He's gone now and you're all
right."

"Dead . . . is he dead?"

"Not dead, just run off. He will be dead soon.
I'm going after him."

"Fiddler, is that you?"

"Sure as shooting. Sure as shooting. God, I'm
glad I found you, McCan. He was going to . . ."

I faded out again and heard no more. When I
awakened, the fire had burned down to embers and
the camp was empty except for me. I lay still for
a long time, my left hand pumping agony up my
arm with every beat of my pulse. Slowly I sat up,
then rose, and with my head swimming, I staggered
to where I had left my horse. It was still there.

Somehow I managed to get into the saddle. Leaning over my saddle horn, my shattered hand pressed to my belly, I rode.

It was no longer dark, and beneath me was a soft feather tick, not the hard earth of Big Jim's camp. Sunlight poured in through a window to my right, and I didn't hurt anymore. After five minutes of staring at the ceiling, I slowly turned my head to the left and saw my hand, splinted and bound tightly in crisp white cloth.

A door opened and a slump-shouldered man with white hair and a pale face came to my bedside. "Hello, son," he said. "My name is Arnold York. I'm a doctor."

"You didn't cut it off."

"What's that?"

"You didn't cut off my hand."

He smiled with one side of his mouth, the other apparently stiffened by apoplexy. "No, I didn't. I thought it might prove useful to you to keep it."

"I feared I'd lose it."

"What happened to you, son?"

"An Indian. He tied me down and smashed my hand."

The doctor's eyes widened. "You're telling me there's some sort of Indian trouble about? I've heard of nothing like that."

"Just one Indian. He thought I knew something he wanted to know." I closed my eyes and smiled. "I feel good, Doc."

"You ought to. I've got you so opiated you ought to be floating on the brink of heaven."

"Where am I?"

"Miles City. This is my office."

"How'd I get here?"

"You rode in about sunrise. You were in a bad way. You've been sleeping all day."

"I want to sleep some more."

"Go ahead. It's the best thing for you—but drink some water first. You're dried out."

I managed a few sips. Drug-induced weariness began to crawl over me; as I drifted off again, I thought of Maggie, Vera Ann, and Longhurst, and wondered if all was well with them. Then I remembered Fiddler, heading off into the night to kill Big Jim. None of the thoughts brought me worry, for the doctor's medicines had robbed me of the ability to fret over anything. It was a blessed, needed relief.

By the next morning, pain was with me again—and so was Longhurst. He was at my bedside when I awakened.

"McCan, are you all right?" Longhurst's usual teasing tone was absent; he looked sincerely worried about me. I found it gratifying.

"I'll live, or so the doctor says. How much use of this hand I'll have I don't yet know. How's Maggie?"

"Fine. I rode like the devil after you sent me off and got to her in good time. Fiddler never showed up, and neither did Big Jim. Now tell me what happened with you."

I filled him in. Telling the story brought it all back clearly and made me realize how close to a slow and painful death I had come. Fiddler Smith truly had proven to be my guardian angel. Any hard feelings I had toward him were gone now; he had more than made up for abandoning me to that saloon mob outside Walden City.

"What I don't know is what happened between Fiddler and Big Jim after I rode off," I said. "Fiddler went off swearing to track him down and kill him."

"I'll see what I can find out," Longhurst said. "If there was a killing, there'll be a body, and those usually have a way of turning up, in my experience. The thing for you to do now is to not worry about anything but getting healed up."

"I want to see Maggie."

"She'll want to see you, too. When I told her you'd gone off looking for Fiddler Smith, she got fretful. But she doesn't know yet about you being hurt. I didn't know, either, until I rode back down to find out about you. When you weren't at the ranch, I came into town and asked around until I traced you down."

"Go back to her, Longhurst. Tell her I'm fine, and I'll be up to see her at first chance."

"I will. Reckon running the L&M Ranch is going to have to take a back seat for a few days, huh?"

"Reckon so."

"I'll be back to see you. You rest. The doctor tells me he's going to let you go soon, so you be patient, hear?"

Longhurst left. I lay there wishing I had thought to ask him to roll a cigarette for me, for I couldn't manage it myself with one hand bandaged up. In all my days on roundups, I had never learned the near-essential cowboy skill of rolling a smoke one-handed.

The doctor let me go the next afternoon, with stern instructions not to try to use my injured hand until he gave the say-so. Maggie wanted me to come back to Upchurch to continue my rest, and tempting though that sounded, I had to turn her down. My place was at the ranch, far too neglected these past days. So from Miles City we rode out to the L&M. Maggie sat close to me on the wagon seat, gently holding my injured hand in hers. The nightmare I had been through in Big Jim's camp seemed minor compared with the happiness and hope for the future that Maggie's unveiled concern gave me.

Vera Ann, for some reason, was silently tearful and said nothing to me at all. As for Longhurst, he looked weary and solemn all the way. I attributed that to his extensive back-and-forth travel between Miles City and Upchurch, but when we were at the ranch, he pulled me aside and gave me news that explained both his somber manner and Vera Ann's emotional state.

"Yesterday I found where Big Jim's camp had been," he told me. "I scouted around, looking for sign of what might have happened after you got away. Not a quarter-mile off, I found where they must have met up again and fought. There was blood on the ground." He stopped a moment and swallowed. "And an ear."

I gaped, "An ear . . ."

"Yes. A white man's ear. No bodies—just the ear."

I had to sit down. "So Big Jim got Fiddler instead of Fiddler getting him." The thought saddened me. "You figure Fiddler is dead?"

"I do. Most likely Big Jim hid the corpse somewhere. I guess cutting off the ear was his way of marking the job done. The only thing I can't figure is why he didn't take it with him. It seems the kind of thing a man like that would do, you know.''

"Vera Ann's taking it hard?''

"Real hard. I think she's decided she liked Fiddler Smith a lot more than she had thought.''

"I know the feeling,'' I replied. "I really do.'' I stood and took a deep breath. "Fiddler wasn't a saint, but it's sad to me to think of him dead, especially after saving my life like he did.''

"What's done is done, McCan. We can take some comfort, at least, in all that trouble being over now. With Fiddler gone, that should be the last we see of Big Jim, and for that we can all say good riddance. Now come on—let's cook these women some supper.''

PART THREE

FIDDLER'S RETURN

Chapter 18

In every man's life there are many occasions when nothing goes as it should and every plan and dream shatters. Much more rare are those times when the dreams come true and the plans become reality, as if by magic. Rare times—but they do come, once, maybe twice, in the life of every man. The weeks following my encounter with Big Jim were such a time for me.

I suppose it was a new awareness of my mortality, prompted by my ordeal, that led me to evaluate my life and opportunities. Already my love for Maggie was fully reborn; now it blossomed. Beyond a doubt I knew that I wanted her for my wife, just as I had years ago. In those days she had seen me as only a friend. Now, I hoped, she would see me as more.

I remembered the frustration of watching her being taken from me the first time largely because I had assumed too much and acted too slowly. This time I wouldn't make that mistake. A mere month after my painful brush with Big Jim, I asked Maggie to become my wife . . . and she said yes.

Maggie's marriage ceremony to Rodney Upchurch had been a massive outdoor affair, appropriate to his station as a successful merchant. We opted for a quieter, smaller ceremony. In a tiny shingled chapel a few miles from the Emporium, I stood straight and proud with Maggie, Longhurst "best-manning it," to use his terminology, at my side. A few words from the preacher, and suddenly Luke McCan was transformed from a lonely, gambling drifter to the husband of the prettiest lady on the plains of Montana.

We returned to the Emporium after the ceremony, to enjoy a small, unpretentious reception. Longhurst meandered over and congratulated me, though in a downcast way. I pressed him to find what was wrong. "How the blazes am I supposed to run a cattle operation with my partner living a dang forty million miles away and all preoccupied with his sweetheart?" he asked me.

"You're exaggerating things just a little, Longhurst. You're going to find life easier, not harder."

"Huh! I'd like to believe that one!"

"Believe it. Maggie's a woman of some money, and she's offered to bolster up the ranch until things start ticking on their own—in other words, Longhurst, you can go hire yourself Stewart Biggs and maybe even a couple more to do your work for you."

Such a look of surprise and relief I've never seen. Longhurst kissed my bride, not bothering to ask my permission, and wandered off to spike the punch, take a few snorts of snuff, and talk boisterously to Vera Ann. She hardly said a word back to him and didn't even smile. Not that I had expected her to; she had been a sad young woman of late, and with good reason. She had first lost a father, then also the man who wanted to be her husband. All that lay before her now was a struggle to birth and raise a child without a husband to support her. I can't honestly say I liked Vera Ann, but I did feel sorry for her.

The demands of the L&M ranch and the Upchurch Emporium together made a honeymoon for Maggie and me impossible. Our first night was spent in Maggie's house behind the Emporium (now my house, too—the idea took some getting used to) in a new bedroom built on the east end. Maggie and I had agreed it would be best to begin our married life in a chamber unshadowed by personalities and sorrows now past. I wouldn't begrudge Maggie her fond memories of Rodney Upchurch, any more than she would begrudge my memories of Cynthia. Even so, we saw no reason to let those memories become a potential burden on our relationship.

These were happy days, if busy ones. Longhurst did hire Biggs and a couple of other hands, but it was still often necessary for me to travel back and forth between Upchurch and the L&M. Nevertheless, I had no complaints about it. I was married to my old love and nothing could dampen the joy of that.

Nothing, I should say, except Vera Ann Walden. The poor girl, growing bigger and slower by the week as her pregnancy advanced, reminded me of a comic picture I had once seen of a sad old woman who carried a rain cloud with her wherever she went. Vera Ann moped and cried and generally got in the way, and the times Maggie and I most wanted privacy were the times she demanded the most of Maggie's attention. Maggie, bless her, never complained about the burden, although it clearly was wearing her down.

For my part, I worried about what would happen once the baby was born. Would Vera Ann then remain in our home? She had no prospects of a livelihood on her own, and now that Fiddler was gone, no one was about who showed any inclination to take on her care. The situation seemed hopeless.

Weeks became months as the year slid past. Autumn came and brought the chill of a coming winter. Vera Ann fell sick as the end of her pregnancy neared; Maggie at last broke down and confessed she needed help in caring for her. I promptly advertised for a maid and hired the first person to respond: a skinny former schoolteacher with black hair pinned in a pie-shaped roll atop her head. She talked in a tightly clipped, high voice, wore spectacles, had neither lips nor hips, and, to top it off, was named Ambrosia Flatt. "Miss Flatt will be fine," she answered when I asked her what we should call her.

What Miss Flatt lacked in looks and personality she made up for in skill. She moved into Maggie and Rodney's old bedroom, took over much of the cooking and cleaning, and proved an excellent nurse for Vera Ann. Bit by bit the lines that had appeared beneath Maggie's eyes went away and life in our house became more pleasant, even if more crowded.

Longhurst met Miss Flatt on a Sunday afternoon when he came in for a visit and supper. I was both amazed and secretly amused to see he was immediately smitten with our new maid. "I'll be coming up to see you more often," he told me before he left. "There's no reason for you to be riding out to the L&M so much, with all you've got to do here."

I smiled. Taylor Longhurst never volunteered for any extra exertion unless he had something to gain.

Maggie received the telegram from Bozeman the very afternoon that Vera Ann went into her travails. A Bozeman cousin on her late mother's side was very ill and required her help. Maggie, usually a staunch woman, couldn't restrain her tears at the prospect of leaving home for an indefinite period. Just lately life had started being what we had hoped it would be—and now this.

We had no time to talk the situation over that day, because of Vera Ann's labor. Maggie and Miss Flatt stayed at Vera Ann's side throughout the all-night birthing. I didn't even go to bed; Vera Ann's screams and moans wouldn't have let me sleep anyway. I couched myself into a chair in the sitting room and smoked the night away. At last weariness overcame all else and I drifted off a little before sunrise.

Maggie shook me awake an hour later. She looked haggard but happy. "It's a girl," she said. "Healthy and fat and strong."

I smiled. "I'm thankful. How's Vera Ann?"

"Exhausted, but well enough. She's sleeping. She named the baby Martha."

"Martha . . . like my sister."

"That's who she named her after."

I was touched. Vera Ann had heard me talk often of my late sister from Independence; naming her child after her must have been Vera Ann's way of thanking me for the roof I had put over her head in a difficult time. Hard feelings I had aplenty for Vera Ann, but from that moment on they were substantially tempered.

Soon enough I would have reason to be glad for the softening of my attitude. Vera Ann was already a tragic figure to me; before long an even greater tragedy would descend upon her, one none of us could anticipate at that time.

I drove Maggie to Miles City the next day and she boarded a Northern Pacific train for Bozeman. "Don't be sad," she told me. "I'm not that far away by train."

"Any distance is too far," I replied. "I don't have a good feeling about you going off. The last time folks I care about climbed on a train, I never saw them again."

Her eyes flashed. "Don't say that," she said firmly. "Don't even think a thought like that. I'll be back, soon."

The train smoked and chugged as it pulled away from the station. I watched it until it was out of sight. My bad feeling lingered. I felt that trouble was on its way, and I hoped as hard as I could that it would not find Maggie.

Turning away, I returned to the buggy and drove up onto Main Street to the nearest cafe, for I had not eaten for hours. I was so low I didn't even taste the meal, good food though it was. From Miles City I rode out to the L&M to check on matters there. Longhurst didn't know I was coming—otherwise I'm sure he would have been out working with the hired men, rather than lounging back in a wicker-bottomed chair on the porch, writing on a pad of paper.

He stood quickly when I rode up, dropping the

pad behind him on the chair and looking embarrassed.

"Working hard, I see."

"Now, McCan, don't you talk smart-mouth to me. What I'm doing is important . . . at least to me. What are you doing here?"

I told him about Maggie's call to Bozeman, and about the birth of Vera Ann's baby. "Miss Flatt's taking good care of mother and child. I'm glad we hired her," I commented.

"Me too," he said.

I stayed the night at the ranch house. Longhurst went back to work on his pad right after supper, scribbling erasing, scribbling again until late in the night. The next morning he self-consciously handed me an envelope. "Give this to Miss Flatt, would you?"

"What is it—a love letter?"

"Mind your own business, Luke McCan."

The wind was up and kicking with the dawn, and blasted me all the long way back to Upchurch. I had tucked Longhurst's envelope into a coat pocket; a particularly powerful gust swept it out. Papers scattered and blew, and only with much exertion was I able to chase them down, all the while cussing at Longhurst for failing to seal his envelope.

I didn't deliberately try to read Longhurst's private correspondence, but stuffing the papers back into the envelope I couldn't help seeing what he had written. It was, of all things, a poem.

"Ambrosia, Ambrosia, name as sweet as honey, I'd rather look upon your face as find a pot of money . . ." Then farther down: "If I was a flower, I'd like to be a posey, and get plucked up by the roots and smelt by sweet Ambrosey . . .''

I was right: Longhurst was in love. Nothing but love could make a man write fool verse like that and think it good. I didn't know what effect the poem would have on Ambrosia Flatt, but it certainly lifted my spirits. I laughed out loud most of the way back to Upchurch.

Chapter 19

I dreamed about Fiddler Smith that night. Back in Walden City we were, in that little shack of a house Ike Walden had provided us. Fiddler was grinning around his secret whiskey bottle, reaching under that leather patch to scratch at the nub where an ear once had been, and rattling on about the wonder of women. He picked up his fiddle, drew the bow across the caked strings, and began to sing in that distinctive voice: "Love somebody and I do, I do, love somebody and I do . . ."

I awakened depressed. Sitting up in the dark room, I put my hand over to touch Maggie, only then remembering she was not there. At the moment, that was too much to abide. I rose, put on a pair of trousers and a shirt, and headed to the kitchen to roust up a midnight feast.

I was finishing off some cold ham slabs on bread when Vera Ann appeared at the door. She was wrapped up in one of Maggie's old robes, a thick woolen shroud Maggie had loaned her. Vera Ann smiled and nodded hello, then came and sat down across from me at the table. The lamplight spilling onto her face showed the subtle lines and crevices that had come onto her features over the past nine months. Ordeals always leave tracks, and Vera Ann had been trod upon by her share.

"Hungry?" I asked her.

"A little."

I shoved the plate toward her. "You take the rest. I'm satisfied."

"I dreamed about Fiddler," she said abruptly.

"Really? That's a funny thing—I did the same."

"Was yours a good dream?"

"Sad, mostly. It's always sad to me to dream about somebody and wake up and remember they're dead."

"Mine was a good dream." Her eyes were wistful, staring into the lamp flame, then rising to meet mine. "I don't believe he's dead."

"Vera Ann, you know as well as I do that—"

"Finding Fiddler's ear doesn't mean he's dead. An ear isn't a corpse. Fiddler had one ear cut off years ago, and he didn't get killed that time. Maybe it happened again."

I had my doubts, but said nothing.

"I believe he's alive," she reaffirmed. "I believe he'll come back to me."

"If he's alive, I think he would have already come back," I said gently. "The night he and the Indian fought, Fiddler was out looking for me because he thought he could find you if he found me. Likely he was jealous, too, thinking I had taken in a woman he saw as his. Feelings that strong wouldn't have just left him. If he had lived through that fight, he would have kept hunting until he found you."

She looked back to the flame again, her face more somber. "I don't care what anyone thinks," she said very softly. "Fiddler's alive, and he'll come back for me."

She rose and walked out of the kitchen and back toward her room. She had not touched the food on the plate.

Christmas came and went and Maggie still had not returned. Her cousin's ailment, from what I could tell from her letters, was centered in her lungs, was getting no worse, yet getting no better either. Thus Maggie was left in a limbo with no foreseeable end. The second day of the new year brought me a new letter from Maggie, with a despairing plea: Please come and see me, as soon as you can. I miss you terribly.

I smiled. Even before receiving the letter I had already decided to go see Maggie; being without her was becoming too much to bear. Her plea only made me more eager to go.

I almost missed the postscript at the end of the letter, for the paper had folded in such a way as to nearly hide it. When I read it, I rose from my chair, amazed. "P.S.—I think I saw Fiddler Smith in Bozeman today."

That's all it said.

Fiddler . . . alive? Could Vera Ann's intuition have been correct?

I stood debating about whether to tell Vera Ann about the postscript. She was down in the Emporium today, having begun working there, at her own request, a few hours each week. No, I decided. No point in getting up her hopes based on something this insubstantial. Maggie had never laid eyes on Fiddler Smith and knew him only by description. Probably she had seen someone else.

Longhurst arrived that afternoon. He came to Upchurch much more frequently than he used to, now that he and Ambrosia Flatt were courting. His poem had done the trick. After I delivered it to her—struggling to keep my composure—she had gone through some remarkable changes. Silence gave way to chatter, sternness to cheerfulness. And she started to eat—eat a lot. The results were initially positive—"rounding off the Flatt real nice and pretty," as Longhurst punned—but the woman was showing no signs of slowing down her consumption, and was starting to grow too plump. Romance gave her an appetite.

I told Longhurst of my coming journey to Bozeman and asked him to remain at Upchurch during my absence. "To see to the store, you know, and make sure Vera Ann and Miss Flatt are safe and sound." As I said it, I thought of the old saw about asking the wolf to guard the henhouse—but what choice did I have?

"I'll be glad to stay," he said. "I'll set up my cot down in the side room at the Emporium."

"Thanks. There's something else I want to mention to you, by the way. I got a letter from Maggie. She says she thinks she might have seen Fiddler Smith in Bozeman. That's all it said—no details."

"I'll be! Reckon it could be true?"

"Anything's possible, I suppose. I can't quite believe it, and I haven't said anything to Vera Ann, so don't mention it. While I'm in Bozeman I might check around and see what I can find out."

*　　*　　*

Bozeman was a fine and appealing Gallatin Valley town—the "Garden of Montana," some called it—that guarded the entrance to those vast mountains that rumple the western third of Montana and the upper portions of Idaho. It was named after John M. Bozeman, the famous trailmaker, and had quite a lively history. You might recall it as the town where back in 1873 vigilantes strung up "Old Man Tripp" Triplett and "Steamboat Bill" St. Clair to a beef dressing rack. Likely as not you've seen the photograph.

Maggie was waiting for me at the station when the Northern Pacific train finally screeched and steamed to a halt. What a sight she was! I hugged her until she expressed fear for the survival of her ribs. I hardly let her get the protest out before I cut it off with a kiss, and us right there on the platform where everyone could see us.

Maggie had brought her cousin's rockaway to pick me up in. We took the roundabout route back to the house, Maggie showing me the town, with its wide streets and nice brick buildings. A long team of freight wagons was rolling down Main Street as we went up it; the sight took me back to my old days of freighting between Pierre and Deadwood back in Dakota. It was good to see freighters at work; since the growth of the railroads, there was much less of that old-fashioned type of conveying going on.

"How's Freida?" I asked, Freida being Maggie's cousin.

"Better today—I'm hopeful of returning home soon, if she holds up."

"Lord have mercy, I hope she does. I've missed you terrible."

She asked about Vera Ann and the baby, and about Miss Flatt. I told her all were fine, and prompted a laugh from her when I described the growing romance between Longhurst and our housekeeper. "I just hope Longhurst will behave himself while I'm gone," I said.

"How does Vera Ann do with the baby?"

"She keeps it fed, and loves it dear . . . but beyond that it's Miss Flatt who gives most of the care. Vera Ann's not the most, well, competent mother I've seen. She's hardly more than a child herself, in some ways."

Freida Davenworth's house, just off Main Street, was a fine dwelling. Freida's husband had been a successful rancher who sold out at just the right time to reap a good profit and set his wife up in a fine home before drinking himself to death. Alcohol poisoning, the doctor had called it. Freida, childless, lived now on the substantial savings her husband had put by, and I admit I resented that she had called Maggie in to help her instead of hiring a nurse. Maggie had chided me for feeling that way, reminding me that we really couldn't know Freida's financial circumstances, and had to assume she spoke truly when she said she couldn't afford bought help.

Freida was sitting up in bed, looking pale but cheery in a sunny yellow gown and robe. She had me shake her wilted stem of a hand and told me how kind Maggie had been to her, and that soon Maggie would be able to return home to me. I hope so, I replied.

Maggie and I shared supper and stories that evening in the kitchen. In the midst of it all I recalled her mysterious reference to having seen Fiddler Smith.

To my surprise, she shuddered. "It was a horrible thing," she said. "I had decided not to even mention it to you, then on an impulse I scribbled that note at the end. Yes, I'm sure it was Fiddler Smith. It had to be."

"Where did you see him?"

"In a barroom . . . don't look at me like that—I didn't go in. I saw him through the door."

"What was the 'horrible thing'?"

"The night I saw Fiddler Smith, I was nearly robbed . . . maybe even worse. It was my fault, in a way. I shouldn't have gone where I did.

"It was evening, and I was out walking. Caring for Freida can be exhausting, and sometimes I just have to get away. I wandered too far and got onto a street at the far end of town. Nothing but saloons and a couple of dance halls. When I saw what I had stumbled into, I turned and started for home . . . then I heard music. The sweetest music I had heard for so long. It was a violin, playing something that sounded maybe Irish or Scottish, very pretty and sad.

"I know it sounds foolish, but I had to see where that music was coming from. I turned back around and went further up the street. Some men stepped out from beside one of the saloons and walked behind me, getting closer all the time. I walked faster, they walked faster . . . then I reached another one of the saloons and somebody opened the door. That was where the music was coming from. The door was only open for a couple of moments, but it was long enough for me to see who was playing that violin. A tall man, thin. And he had no ears at all.

He had grown his hair long and let it hang down the sides of his head to cover it, but you could still tell.

"I knew right away it had to be Fiddler Smith. I was surprised, but there wasn't time to think about it, not with those men behind me. I started to run, and they ran right after me. Almost caught me."

"My lord, Maggie!" I said, heart pounding. "How did you get away?"

"Some other men stopped them. There are gentlemen of sorts even in a place like that, it seems. I suppose they didn't like seeing a woman chased. I didn't stay around to say thank you. I ran all the way back to Freida's house, and never said a word about what happened."

I reached out to her and hugged her close. I remembered my bad feeling about her coming to Bozeman and wondered if it had resulted from some premonition of that evening of danger for Maggie. Thank God she had come through all right.

"I'm staying here with you until you can come home," I said, announcing a decision made on the spot. "I'll not have us separated any more. I'll wire Longhurst in the morning and let him know."

"But who will run the Emporium?"

"Longhurst and Vera Ann can handle it. Stewart Biggs can keep the L&M running without Longhurst about—it's winter, after all, and Biggs has really been running the operation anyway."

Maggie smiled and kissed me. "I'm glad you're staying," she said. "I've missed you so badly."

"You don't have to miss me anymore."

That night, for the first time in far too long, I

slept with my wife at my side, and I felt like one of those biblical lame men made whole again. But in the back of my mind I kept wondering if that really had been Fiddler Smith Maggie had seen. I had to know, and I determined that before I left Bozeman, know I would. I would go to that street, find that saloon, and if Fiddler Smith was there, I would meet him and learn what happened that night after he saved my hide from Big Jim.

I rolled over, put my arm around Maggie, and went to sleep.

Chapter 20

I strode down the street and turned onto an avenue of run-down structures long ago claimed by equally run-down specimens of humanity. It was like a hundred other rows of dives and vice dungeons I had known in my day. Once I had been a part of this kind of world; now I felt a stranger. Luke McCan, I realized, had been changed much by marriage and responsibility, and I was glad of it.

Two drunks staggered past, jostling me without apology, probably hardly realizing I was there. They stank of liquor and sweat. Stepping over a big gap in the boardwalk, I studied the doors of the various saloons and wondered if I would find Fiddler Smith beyond one of them. Pulling my coat around me in the cold wind, I picked one tavern at random and made for the entrance.

Plenty of men inside, and a few human beings that once might have been ladies, but no Fiddler. I exited and made for the next saloon and had no better results there, nor in the next one. Walking onto the street, I considered giving up and heading home, when a most remarkable event occurred.

The next saloon down had a large window of red-and-white checkerboard glass. As I paused to roll a cigarette—still difficult because my injured hand remained stiff and nearly useless—that window exploded outward, and a big man tumbled onto the boardwalk. I leaped back. He lay there stunned, then rose groggily. He was hardly on his feet before another figure came through the window on a leap. It was none other than Fiddler Smith himself, fiddle and bow still in hand. He let out a roar and kicked the dazed man, knocking him onto his rump. Another kick sent him rolling into the street.

"Fiddler!" I exclaimed, stepping forward. A bad move—Fiddler turned and kicked again, his heel digging into my gut and doubling me over.

Three others emerged from the saloon, two by the door, one by the now-glassless window. I rolled to the side, trying to find my breath again, as Fiddler Smith became embroiled in a very major scuffle. The fiddle dropped and was crushed beneath a boot. Fiddler cursed, and gouged the crusher in the eye with the tip of the bow, snapping it. That put that man out of commission, but left Fiddler still facing the other two, one of whom had a knife.

By now I had managed to get to my feet again. Without a thought I waded in, swinging my fists and bringing down the knife-wielder. I stomped his wrist, stooped, and grabbed the knife, which I tossed onto the roof of the saloon. Fiddler, meanwhile, was pounding away at the remaining man, giving and receiving about an equal amount of damage. I joined him from behind. Balling my fists together, I brought them down on the brawler's head and knocked him to his knees. Fiddler let out a laugh and kneed the man on the chin.

"Come on!" I urged. "Let's get out of here!"

He only then saw who I was. "McCan! What the . . ."

"Run!" I shouted, for others were coming out the door toward us.

Quite a parade it was, Fiddler and I running down the boardwalk, pursued by three rowdies who looked twice as big as they probably really were. I don't mind confessing that it was mortal fear that drove me down that boardwalk, knocking over several unfortunate stragglers who got in the way at the wrong time. Fiddler and I rounded the corner onto Main and ran all the harder, until at last our pursuers fell away, waved us off with curses and bluster, and strode breathless back the way they had come.

Fiddler and I went a little farther and cut into an alley, where we leaned side by side against a wall, panting. Fiddler began to laugh.

"Fiddler and McCan, back at it again!" he declared. "Lord a'mercy, McCan, where in the devil did you come from?"

"I've been looking for you," I said. "My wife is here, and she said she saw you . . . aw, forget it for now. It's a long story, and I can tell it better sitting down."

"Come on, then," Fiddler said. "I'll buy you a whiskey."

"Make it a cup of coffee," I said. "I'm a more respectable soul than I used to be."

"All right, Saint Luke. Coffee it is. There's a cafe right across the street yonder."

"Sorry about what happened to your fiddle," I said.

"Forget about it. It went out like I want to, scrapping and gouging. My daddy would have been proud."

Fiddler had never been much to look at, but with both ears missing he was downright ugly. He wore no patches to cover either hole, and his longer hair didn't really hide the deformities all that well. "You'd be surprised how hard of hearing it makes a fellow when his ears are gone," he said. "When I put patches over 'em I can't hear a dang thing."

"I'm glad to find you alive," I said. "I had thought that Big Jim killed you. I owe you my life."

"You don't owe me," he said. "Ain't nobody in the world that owes this sorry old beggar a thing. Now tell me what you're doing here."

I told him about my marriage to Maggie, about her ailing cousin and her trip to Bozeman, and how she had spotted Fiddler inside the saloon. "I had to come and find you, and say thanks for what you did for me."

"Thanks accepted, if you got to give it. But like I said, you don't owe me a thing. You've helped me, and I helped you."

"What was all that ruckus over back yonder?"

"Nothing. One of them fellows took to calling me 'Earless Smith' and it riled me. You know how I am."

"I do. Now start talking. I want to know what happened with you and Big Jim that night."

"I killed him, that's what," he said. "I think I did, at least. I sure 'nough put a bullet in him."

He took a swallow of coffee, smacked his lips, and told his story, starting from the time he fled

Powderville after I warned him about Big Jim.

"Hearing Big Jim was that close put a scare into me, and I headed for Dakota. I got no farther than Glendive before I stumbled into some work, helping build a big horse barn. I kind of liked it there, and Big Jim never showed up, so I got it in mind that I might just settle in Montana. Then this drifter came through from Miles City. He was a big talker, this one. He said there was a new cattle operation over near Miles City, run by a man named McCan and a partner. I told him I knew you, and that's when he told me that you had took in some pregnant woman who passed out on the street. I figured it right off to be Vera Ann.

"I'll admit it square: it made me mad to think of Vera Ann being with you. Jealousy, I reckon. The way this fellow told it, it sounded like she was living with you, you know, like a wife. I fumed over it until it got the best of me, and got on my horse and went to Miles City to find you, not knowing that Big Jim had sniffed me out again and was right on my tail. I got drunk in town, made a little too much ruckus, and had to run. I had heard that your ranch was west of town, and headed out that way to find you. And find you I did, all staked out in Big Jim's camp. You know what happened from there."

"It's what happened after that I really want to know."

"Not a lot to tell. I tracked down Big Jim and we fought. He got me down, sliced off this other ear of mine, and was set to cut my throat when I got my hand on my pistol—I'd dropped it during the scuffle. I put a bullet into his side and he scampered off. I must have passed out, for when I came to, he was long gone. I looked for him and never found him.''

''So you don't really know he's dead.''

''No . . . but he's got to be. That was a bad wound I give him. And he never came back. I think he crawled off into a hole and died.''

''There was no body found—my partner looked. All he found was blood on the ground, and your ear.''

''Well, I can't explain it. But I still think he's dead.''

''I hope he is, for your sake.''

Fiddler grinned. ''That kind of talk makes a man nervous.''

''Sorry. You know me—I worry a lot. But tell me, why didn't you come to find me when it was all over?''

Fiddler shook his head thoughtfully. ''Don't know that I can answer that. All I can tell you is that as I sat out there nursing this chopped-off ear stump, I had time to sober up and think. I started seeing things different. I figured Vera Ann was better off without me, that she was probably happier being with you. So I patched up my ear, said my good riddances to Big Jim, and started riding west. I wound up here in Bozeman, and have been here ever since.''

''Vera Ann never was with me, not like you were thinking,'' I said. ''I took her up to Upchurch and asked Maggie to take her in. She's had her baby now, Fiddler. A fat little girl she named Martha, after my sister.''

Fiddler's eyes went moist. ''Martha. That's a fine name. I'm glad to hear about it . . . I feel like she's half mine, even though I really wasn't her father.''

"So come and see her. I think Vera Ann would be glad to see you, too.''

"What's she doing now?''

"Clerking at Maggie's store a little. That's about it. She still lives with us.''

"Vera Ann,'' he said, just to hear the name. "Vera Ann.''

"Come back to Upchurch with me, Fiddler. Come meet that baby.''

"I can't.''

"Why not?''

"Because if I see Vera Ann, I'll want to marry her, and that can't ever be. I ain't fit to be a husband, much less a father. She's better off alone than with me. Hell, McCan, you know how it is with me. Everybody I get close to I bring trouble to. It's always been that way.''

I didn't know how to respond to that, so I said, "She'll at least be glad to hear you're alive. All this time we've been thinking Big Jim killed you. She's resisting believing it. She dreamed about you the other night, she told me. Dreamed you were alive and so now she really believes you are . . . and me all the while trying to make her believe you're dead. I guess the joke's on me.''

"The only joke here is sitting in front of you. Keep on telling Vera Ann I'm dead until she believes it. It's for the best.''

I crushed out my cigarette, dismayed to see how low an opinion Fiddler had developed about himself. It was downright saddening. "All right,'' I said. "I won't tell her, if that's the way you really want it.''

"It is."

We parted shortly after. I watched Fiddler Smith's lean figure stride off in the darkness. I felt sorry for him, sorry for Vera Ann, and sorry for little Martha, whose future seemed so unsure. What would become of her, growing up fatherless?

That thought stayed on my mind all the way back to the house, where Maggie awaited me.

"Did you find him?"

"I found him."

"I knew it had to be him, I knew it!"

"I asked him to come back with us. He said no. And he doesn't want us to tell Vera Ann he's alive."

"Why?"

"He thinks it's better that way. But you know, Maggie, I believe he still loves Vera Ann. He just thinks himself too worthless to have her." I sat down beside her. "I've been thinking. I want us to ask Vera Ann if we can adopt Martha. Raise her as our own. What would you think about that?"

Maggie smiled. "I think it's a wonderful idea, Luke McCan. And I think you're a wonderful man for thinking it."

She kissed me. The touch of her, the scent of her, filled me with warmth. I stood, swept her up like she was a child, carried her to our room, and closed the door behind us.

Chapter 21

Maggie and I returned home by the Northern Pacific two weeks later, after Freida rallied and declared herself fit for normal living. I had not seen Fiddler Smith since that one encounter, and as Bozeman disappeared behind us, I expected never to lay eyes on him anymore. All the way home I thought about him, and about Vera Ann's determined belief that he was alive and would return to her. She had been right about the first part, not the second. Fiddler had convinced me he would never come back for Vera Ann.

He was right, I decided. It is best that she keep on thinking he's dead. Better that she feel the pain of loss instead of the pain of rejection—though from Fiddler's viewpoint, he wasn't rejecting Vera Ann by declining to come for her. He was rejecting himself.

We found the Emporium and the L&M all operating in fine form, though the store was dirty and sloppy from Longhurst's overly easygoing management. As for the L&M, its temporary loss of Longhurst during my absence was actually its gain; Stewart Biggs had been running things and doing a better job of it than Longhurst ever had.

Vera Ann looked fitter, slimmer, and healthier than when last I had seen her, and the baby had grown like a summer weed, apparently racing the now-rotund Ambrosia Flatt to see who could put on weight the fastest. Miss Flatt had a strong lead. She also had her ring firmly through Longhurst's nose; his heart-on-his-sleeve devotion to her was as strong as ever. He had been living in the side room of the Emporium, no doubt spending more time courting Miss Flatt than doing any honest work.

He wasn't all that happy to see me return, for that meant his time at Upchurch was over and it was back to the L&M for Taylor Longhurst. "I don't cotton much to going," he admitted privately. "I doubt you've noticed it much, but me and Ambrosia have sort of an interest in each other now."

"You don't say. When's the wedding?"

"I ain't asked her . . . yet."

Miss Flatt was depressed after Longhurst left. She moped through her tasks and cared for little Martha without enthusiasm. A woman in love if ever I saw one.

We wasted no time in approaching Vera Ann about the adoption of Martha. I had no idea whether she would react with shock, sorrow, or relief. What we got was a combination of them all—and then, agreement.

"Thank you, Vera Ann," Maggie said. "You can know that Martha is going to be raised in a strong and loving home. We'll treat her as our own child."

Vera Ann smiled the saddest smile I'd ever seen. "And what about me? What will happen to me?"

"Now's not the time to worry over that," I said. "Things will work out right. They most always do."

Things will work out right. They seemed innocent and empty enough words at the time, but they weren't empty. They were filled with irony that would reveal itself only later—irony so bitter it hurts me even as I write it into this narrative.

If only we could see tragedies before they come.

Winter, like a kitten too high in a tree, released its clawing grip with the greatest reluctance. At last the warm winds of spring blew across the plains and the brown land began to turn green. These were the days of rebirth, and the days the trouble came.

A scream awakened me one night, a scream from Vera Ann's room. The voice, however, was not Vera Ann's, but Ambrosia Flatt's. I leaped from my bed, dragged on my trousers and grabbed my pistol, and darted out the door to find out what had happened.

Miss Flatt, holding a lamp in one hand as she pressed the other to the side of her head, stood in the door of Vera Ann's room. A trickle of blood ran down between her fingers. She slumped against the doorframe as I reached her.

"Ambrosia!" I said, in my distraught state forgetting her preferred mode of reference. "What happened?"

She sank to the floor. "He hit me, knocked me cold . . . and now he's taken Martha!"

"Who, Ambrosia? And where's Vera Ann?"

"Gone . . . with him. They were together. He was horrible, ugly . . ." She began to cry. "He had no ears, just ugly holes where ears should be!"

Fiddler. I stepped back, disbelieving. Fiddler Smith had returned after all—returned for his woman and the baby that now legally was mine and Maggie's.

"When did this happen?"

"I don't know . . . I was unconscious for I don't know how long. He hit me! I can't believe he really hit me!"

Maggie showed up; I told her what had happened. "Luke, you've got to go after them! They can't take Martha!"

"Thank God Longhurst is here," I said.

Longhurst was down in the Emporium tonight, having been up to visit Miss Flatt. He had quit bothering with business pretexts for these now-frequent courting journeys. I dressed and hurried down to the Emporium to roust him.

Distant thunder rumbled as I told him what had happened, then a light rain drizzled down, peppering the roof gently as the big Emporium echoed and amplified the sound. "We can't track him in the dark," Longhurst said. "There's nothing to do but wait until first light—then we'll go after him even if it's raining fire and brimstone."

"Why did he come back, Longhurst? Why, after all this time, did he change his mind?"

"Love, that's why. He loves that girl, McCan, and he couldn't stay away from her."

"But why did they have to take Martha? She's not Vera Ann's now—she's ours."

"You got a piece of paper with lawyer writing on it that says she's yours. Vera Ann's got more—she's got her blood in that child's veins. I expect she couldn't find it in her to leave Martha behind."

First light found us mounted and armed. Fiddler

and Vera Ann had taken one of two flatbed wagons that were property of the Emporium, and the tracks were clear on the rain-matted spring grass. Longhurst and I galloped along the path, my optimism growing as we went. Surely we could overtake them.

They were heading north, toward the Missouri. I knew this country well, having traveled it aplenty back in my earlier roaming days. "There's an old line camp up a couple of miles," I said to Longhurst about midday. "Maybe they waited out the storm there. I hope so, for that would help give us a jump on them."

"I been trying to figure, McCan. I don't see how Fiddler can figure he could get away with something like this. He was bound to know he'd be chased—else he wouldn't have gone about things like he did. But why'd he take a wagon? Surely he knows we'd catch up to it."

"He had a woman and baby to haul," I replied. "What else could he do?"

"Something about this don't sit right with me," Longhurst said. "It smells like fish bait sure as this world. I think old Fiddler might be trying to trick us, McCan."

I should have listened to him, for he had lawman instincts, honed by years of tracking and trailing a lot more difficult than what we were doing now. As it was, I didn't even answer him. All I knew was that my adopted baby girl was taken, and the tracks pointed me north. On we rode, toward the river.

The old line camp cabin was so squat and plain that you could pass within a quarter mile of it and never know it was there. Even Longhurst's keen eye might have missed it had it not been for the figure that ran toward us from the cabin's direction. It was Vera Ann, alone and distraught, hands waving above her head as she stumbled toward us.

"Thank God, thank God you've come!" she said, flinging her arms out to hug me hardly before I had time to fully dismount. "If you'll hurry you can stop him—you've got to!"

"What are you talking about, Vera Ann?"

"Fiddler! Oh, Lord help me, he's taken my baby and run off! He's left me here alone!"

I looked at Longhurst and read on his face the same bewilderment I felt. "I don't understand, Vera Ann," I said.

"Fiddler's cast me off," she said, "He came to me in the night—oh, I was so happy to see him alive that at first I thought I was dreaming again—and he told me he had come for me. He said we would be a family, he and Martha and I. But Martha's not mine anymore, I told him. She's adopted by the McCans. Fiddler said it didn't matter, to take her and go away with him. I did it—I know it was wrong, Luke, but I did it.

"We took the wagon and rode in the dark, and at first it was so wonderful—Fiddler talking about the life we would have. But he was drinking while we rode, and he started to change the drunker he got. He talked bad about me, called me terrible names, said I wasn't fit to marry him or care for Martha. When he saw that old cabin yonder he threw me off and rode away with Martha, saying he was bound for Glendive. Oh, Luke, I'm so scared—you've got to go after him and get back Martha!"

"We'll go, all right," I said. "We'll chase him all the way to hell if it takes it. Can you make do in that cabin until we get back?"

"Yes, yes! Please, just go!"

"Hop up behind me on my saddle here and I'll ride you over to the cabin," Longhurst said.

"No!" she declared. "There's no time—just go after Fiddler!"

"She's right," I said. "Come on, Longhurst—we got no time to waste."

Longhurst was looking at Vera Ann in the strangest way, and appeared hesitant to leave. As for me, I was nearly panicked over the thought of a drunken Fiddler Smith having my adopted baby daughter out there on the plains. I wanted to race as hard as we could toward Glendive to intercept him. Longhurst's silent dawdling made me mad.

"In the name of God, Longhurst, let's ride!"

He never took his eyes off Vera Ann. "All right. You're the boss."

We came across Fiddler's wagon tracks again, double furrows through the new grass, and leading from the old line camp on a straight course toward the still-distant community of Glendive. All appeared to be just as Vera Ann had described: her abandoned, Fiddler and the baby gone.

Still Longhurst lagged back, looking around the horizon and back over his shoulder. "What the devil are you looking for, Longhurst?" I bellowed. "We're wasting time!"

"My suspicion exactly," he said. "I think we're making a bad mistake, McCan. I believe Vera Ann was lying to us."

"You're loco," I declared. "Loco and lazy and slow, and if you cause me to lose Fiddler Smith's trail, I'll put a bullet in you, I swear it!''

It was one of the harshest things I had ever said to a man who had done nothing to earn my displeasure. If I had only let him have his say and let his trained instincts guide us instead of my panic, a great tragedy might have been averted.

I know that now. I didn't know it then. We rode on, following Fiddler's wagon tracks.

Chapter 22

Look yonder," Longhurst said, pointing ahead of us. "I see it," I said, squinting my eyes. "Now why do you think Fiddler would abandon the wagon here in the middle of nowhere?"

"Not only abandon it, but take the horse," Longhurst noted.

He was right. The wagon was sitting empty and the horse was gone. I checked the ground and found its tracks, heading northward. I was amazed. What was Fiddler doing—and where was Martha?

Longhurst had dismounted and was also examining the tracks. "It's just like I figured," he said. "He's dumped the wagon, unhitched the horse, and now he's started circling north. He'll cut back to that line camp and get Vera Ann, then the three of them will be off with a fine jump on us. Not a bad plan, huh? He probably had a saddle in the wagon bed. It all makes sense now. I wondered why Fiddler would have told Vera Ann he was going to Glendive if he was really wanting to get rid of her."

"You mean to say he's riding with a baby in his arms?"

"No, no. Fiddler never had Martha out here."

"Where, then?"

"Didn't you notice how keen Vera Ann was to keep me from getting up close to that line camp cabin? Didn't you notice how she ran out to meet us well away from it, and shooed us off before we had a chance to get close enough to hear anything like, say, a kid crying or talking? Heck, he might have even had fresh horses hid around that line camp somewhere, if he planned this out as close as I bet he did."

I could only stand and stare at the north-bound horse tracks and think how gullible I had been. My old Walden City partner had played me like his fiddle, and I had been too panicked to see it.

"We've got to get back to that line camp, then," I said. "They'll have left a trail."

"And we'll be riding worn-out mounts by the time we get back. He's made two idiots out of us, McCan, no denying."

It was so ironic, so hopeless, that I might have laughed . . . except there was nothing funny in the thought of Martha being taken away from me and Maggie. We had grown to love that little girl; she might as well have been flesh and blood of our own.

We mounted and rode back the way we had come, pushing our mounts as hard as we dared, knowing all the while the entire effort might now be futile.

I had expected to find the line camp empty and the tracks of their horses already fading. But as so often happened when Fiddler Smith was about, what I expected wasn't what I got.

They were there, the three of them. Martha was tossing playfully on her back atop a blanket spread on the earth, happily waving chubby little fingers at the clouds. Fiddler sat about ten feet away from her, cradling Vera Ann's bloody head in his lap while he cried. I could see even before I got close that she was dead. There was blood on her chest—the stab wound that had killed her was there—and also on the left side of her neck and down her left shoulder. That blood had streamed down from the place her left ear had been.

Longhurst and I dismounted and walked slowly toward them. Fiddler was weeping like a child, saying over and over again to Vera Ann, just as if she could hear him, that he was sorry, so sorry he had left her. I went over and scooped up Martha, hugging her close and closing my eyes. Thank you, Lord, I prayed. Thank you for keeping my little one safe.

Longhurst went to Fiddler and knelt beside him, examining Vera Ann's corpse. "Big Jim?" he said.

"Yes," Fiddler replied. "Oh, God, oh God, what have I done to my sweet lady? What have I done?"

"You didn't do it," Longhurst said. "It was Big Jim. You couldn't have known he would show up."

"I should have known—I knew he was after me again. But I didn't know he was this close, I truly didn't. I wouldn't have left her if I had. God help me, he got to her before I could double back."

"He must have been close when we were here, McCan," Longhurst said. "He might even have been watching us."

If you've ever seen the top of a Rocky Mountain

pine literally explode into flame in the midst of a big forest fire, you have an idea of the way anger suddenly flared in my mind. It was sparked by a realization that overwhelmed me. I strode forward, grabbed Fiddler by the collar, and pulled him to his feet. Vera Ann's corpse flopped sickeningly to the earth, half-open eyes staring right up at me.

"You mean to tell me you took my baby girl even though you knew Big Jim was after you? What kind of man are you? What kind of trash?" And then I hit him, hard.

Fiddler fell back on his rump with a loud "Oooof!" Sitting there, he closed his eyes and cried even harder. "I deserve it, I do—I want you to shoot me, McCan. I don't deserve to live."

"Reckon you don't. But I'm no murderer."

"Calm down, both of you," Longhurst said. "There's nothing to be gained by nobody shooting nobody. Just be glad the baby's safe—that's the thing to do."

I turned away, rolled a smoke with shaking hands, and let the tobacco fumes settle my nerves. When I turned again, flipping the stub away, Fiddler was sitting by Vera Ann, stroking her hair. It was a pitiful sight. Longhurst was holding Martha, poking her belly with his finger and making her laugh.

I went over and crouched beside Fiddler. "So how long have you known Big Jim was alive after all?"

He sniffed and wiped his sleeve under his nose. "I found out maybe three, four days after you and me talked in Bozeman. I swear I don't know how he lived after the hole I put in him. But he did, and came looking for me."

"How'd he know to look in Bozeman?"

"He didn't. I was on the boardwalk and he was on the back of a prison wagon rolling through Bozeman when we saw each other. We had drifted over into the same parts, and he got himself arrested for one thing or another. The day after I saw him, I heard talk about a big redskin knocking a jailer cold and walking out free. It put a mortal fright into me, for I knew he was coming after me. He found me, too, saw me right across that same street you found me on. I ran like Old Scratch. Stole me the first horse I saw and rode east. I thought I'd shook off Big Jim, really I did.

"That's when I got the notion of coming back to get Vera Ann. She'd been on my mind ever since you talked about her, just weighing on me. So I changed my tune about not coming back to her. I knew she'd never go off with me without her baby, and I had a feeling that if we took the baby you'd chase us. So I came up with this scheme to throw you off track until we could get far away. It would've worked, too . . . except I didn't know Big Jim was so close." He started to weep again. "Why didn't I just let things be? If I'd stayed away, Vera Ann would still be alive."

"I wonder why Big Jim spared the baby?" Longhurst asked. Just hearing the question made me sick to my stomach.

"I think I know," Fiddler said. "I think he didn't know the baby was there. When I found Vera Ann, she was a long way off from the cabin. I believe she ran so he'd chase her and miss the little one."

"Like a mamma quail leading the dogs away from her young," Longhurst said. "What do you think of her doing that!'' He said the last in an admiring tone, looking at Vera Ann's still form.

''I found this on her body,'' Fiddler said. ''He left it for me. He must have known I'd come back.''

He pulled a crumpled paper from his pocket and handed it to me. I unfolded it, swallowed, and read: ''Your woman's life for my family's life. Now the score is even.''

''You understand what this means, Fiddler? He considers it through. He's not going to chase you anymore.''

''I know.'' Fiddler's face hardened like stone. ''Now I'm going to chase him.''

''I figured as much. I'm going with you.''

''No need for that—it's my duty, not yours.''

''Vera Ann Walden lived under my roof. She gave birth to the baby that's now mine—that's right, Fiddler, Maggie and I adopted Martha since last we talked. Vera Ann was murdered, and I won't let the man who murdered her walk away from it.''

Fiddler stood. ''He can't be far away. Let's get started.''

''What weapons you got?''

''A shotgun, yonder with the horse, and this pistol.''

Longhurst stepped up. ''Wait a minute, gents,'' he said. ''We can't go after Big Jim with this youngun to be cared for.''

''No, we can't,'' I replied, ''That's why you're going to take her back to Maggie while Fiddler and I go after Big Jim.''

He protested loudly; he wouldn't be left to tend children while we went after a killer. He was the former lawman, after all; it made more sense for him to go than for me. Martha was my child; it should be me, not him, who took her home.

He made sense, but sense made no difference. I lifted my crippled hand. "It was me who felt Big Jim crush my bones, and who almost had a foot burned off by him. I'm going, Longhurst, and there's no more arguing about it."

He lifted his brows, took in a loud breath through his nostrils, and nodded resignedly. "So it is, then. You take care, Luke McCan."

"I will, don't worry. Get Martha home, quick as you can. And tell Maggie that I'll be back. Tell her not to worry."

"She won't need to worry," Longhurst said. "I'll be doing enough of that to count for everybody."

Longhurst gave Fiddler his horse, a better riding mount than the draft horse Fiddler had been upon. We checked weapons, tightened saddles, and I kissed Martha good-bye. She was fussy now, probably from hunger.

We carried Vera Ann's body back to the line camp and laid it out. Burial would have to wait; now there was neither time nor means for it. Fiddler stroked the hair back off her brow one last time, then turned his back and looked at her no more. We mounted and began our journey, following the sign Big Jim had left.

Side by side Fiddler and I rode, moving east, for the tracks of Big Jim's horse led that way. "He's going toward Glendive, just like you did," I said.

"McCan, I want you to know something," Fiddler said. "I've done plenty of wrong in my day, and I rode with the Independent Army, which was as bad a bunch as I've ever been with. But I swear on my mother's grave, I never killed Big Jim's kin, and I never took his ear. The man that did it blamed it on me when the Sioux caught up with us, trying to keep them from taking their blades to him. Big Jim believed him, for he had been out cold when his ear was cut and never saw the face. He's hated me all these years for a thing I never did.

"I want you to believe that, McCan. It's important to me that you believe it."

I looked in his face in the waning afternoon light. Studying his eyes, I looked for signs of deception and found none. "I believe you," I said. And I really did, then and forever thereafter.

Chapter 23

We rode until the fading light forced us to stop, then spent a nearly sleepless night beneath an intensely black sky. When we awoke the next morning, Fiddler was in a despairing mood. In the previous twilight we had wandered off Big Jim's trail; now there seemed no hope of finding it again.

"We can only go on to Glendive and hope that's really where he's bound," I said. "Though he could have turned off at any point. Do you think he believed you'd come after him?"

Fiddler replied, "He believes it. He knew I couldn't let him kill Vera Ann and just leave him be."

"In that case, he's probably either trying to get as far away as he can . . . or he's planning an ambush."

We made a quick breakfast on some of the bread and dried meat I had brought for Longhurst and myself. I wondered if he had made it safely back with Martha, and hoped that Maggie wouldn't be too worried about what I was doing. It seemed half-loco, when I thought about it. This was between Big Jim and Fiddler . . . no. That was true no longer. The killing of Vera Ann had changed that. It was almost funny—here I was, again championing Vera Ann, just like I had against that harasser back in Walden City. Except now it was too late to do her any good.

In midmorning we saw something far ahead of us on the grasslands. As we drew closer we discovered it was a parked wagon, surrounded by a family in very plain black clothing that marked them as Mennonites. A wheel was off the wagon, but that only partly accounted for them being stuck out here, far from help or shelter. Leaned up against one of the intact wheels was a young man, maybe nineteen or twenty. An older woman, apparently his mother, was squatted beside him, tending to a nasty-looking gash in the side of his head.

The bearded father stepped forward as we rode up. "Do you come for good or for evil?" he asked, and it struck me as a peculiar question.

"For good, I would hope," I replied. "My name's McCan. You appear to be in a fix here."

"We've found misfortune with the breaking of our wheel," he replied in his Iowa Amish accent. "And more misfortune has since found us."

I dismounted and walked over to the injured young man, who was quite dazed. "Did this misfortune come in the form of a big one-eared Indian?"

The man nodded, an expression of surprise on his face. "How do you know this?"

"The story's not worth telling. Suffice it to say we need to find that man. Why did he hit your boy?"

"He was stealing from our wagon, stealing without apology before our very eyes. We had thought he had stopped to help us repair our wheel. Young Zeke grew angry and I'm afraid made himself look threatening. The Indian struck him down. I believe he was unaware of our peaceful ways."

"Peaceful ways and Big Jim the Scarnose are unacquainted with each other," I said. "Which way did he go?"

"From here, north. He had asked us where we were bound, and I told him we were on our way to New Hazelton. He seemed very interested to hear of it, and I think he went looking for it."

"New Hazelton? That's been sitting empty for years."

"We are going to reoccupy it and rebuild it. Others are following us. Forgive me for not identifying myself: I'm William Bund, newly come from Iowa. This is my family."

"Pleased to meet you, Mr. Bund, folks. This man with me is Fiddler Smith. Can we help you set your wagon right?"

"Thank you, sir. You were surely sent of God."

Now that we knew which way Big Jim was going, Fiddler was impatient to head after him. "Keep your shirt on," I side-whispered to him. "It won't take us long to help out these folks."

When the wheel was fixed, I dusted off my hands and asked Bund, "Why would the Indian go toward New Hazelton? Doesn't he know there's nothing there?"

"I don't know, sir," Bund replied. "But I think he might see it as a place to hide. It was my suspicion that he felt pursued—he looked back the way he had come quite a lot." Bund gave us a knowing look. "It was you he was afraid of, maybe?"

"Likely so."

"You are men of the law?"

I nodded. "That's right, or close enough."

"Big Jim's scared," Fiddler said with a tone of satisfaction. "Dogged if he ain't scared of me!"

Bund looked confused. To him I said, "If you think the Indian went to New Hazelton, I advise you to delay going there yourselves until we've had a chance to deal with him."

"I'll heed that. Young Zeke could use the rest, and I have no desire to meet that Indian again."

"Good luck to you, Mr. Bund."

"God bless you, sir."

We mounted and rode north, heading for New Hazelton. Seven or eight years ago the little settlement had been formed by a band of Iowa Mennonites, then abandoned when a plague of illness, followed by a harsh and biting winter, decimated their numbers. Now all that remained was a cluster of empty buildings. The cattlemen had been glad to see the simple agrarian folk leave, cattlemen almost always despising tillers of the earth. Now it appeared New Hazelton was on its way to rebirth.

I had all but forgotten the empty little Mennonite haven. If it was Big Jim's idea to hide there until any potential pursuers went by, I had to give him credit for good thinking. Few would think to look for him there.

"McCan, when the time comes, I want it to be me who kills him," Fiddler said as we drew within two miles of the empty former settlement.

"We'll hope it doesn't come to that," I said. "I'd like to see him stand trial and hang."

"There'll be no judges for Big Jim except me

and almighty God," Fiddler said, "I'll kill him, or he'll kill me, one or the other."

Fiddler crouched, studied the tracks in the earth, then looked up to scan the brown, dreary cluster of buildings that had once been places of shelter and livelihood for a good and faithful people. Now, the fresh tracks told us, they were giving refuge to a man much different than those who had built this place.

"He's here," Fiddler said. "Somewhere in there we'll find him."

My skin seemed to tighten and chill on my frame as I examined the empty community. "Reckon he sees us?"

"Don't know. We'll know he's seen us when we hear the first shot."

"If we live long enough to hear it."

Fiddler turned to me. "Go on back, McCan. You don't belong here. Let me go in and find him."

"We've already been through all that, Fiddler. We're both going."

"You got a family, McCan. I got nothing to lose but a wasted life and too many guilty memories."

"Shut up, Fiddler. I'm going with you."

I unbooted a Winchester from my saddle and Fiddler pulled out a fearsome-looking shotgun. We circled to the west end of the vacant town, where the central street ended right on the grasslands, and entered the town, walking side by side, between our mounts, heads crouched low so he wouldn't be able to get an easy shot at us from any angle. Even so, I felt like a target on legs.

From one end of the street to the other we walked, and nothing happened. At the far end we turned left and went between two buildings. "Where the hell is he?" Fiddler said.

"If he's here, we'll find him . . . or he'll find us."

We changed our tack, leaving the horses in the alley and exploring the town together, guns at ready. Around corners we peered, through doorways, into glassless windows filled with cobwebs. Nowhere was there evidence of human life other than our own.

"I think he's gone, Fiddler," I said.

Fiddler lifted his hand. "Listen!"

I had heard it too. The faint whicker of a horse—on the side of the settlement opposite that where our horses were.

"Let's go," I whispered.

The horse was in a stable; a saddle was tossed over the rail. "So he is here, and hiding," I said.

Fiddler stepped out of the stable into the street. "I feel him," he said in a near-whisper. "He's close . . ."

"Yes," I said, for I felt the same prickle in the skin that Fiddler must have. "It's like I can almost smell him."

Have you ever had something happen to you so abruptly that for a good while you can hardly realize it has happened at all, or even know what has occurred? That was how it was for me when my feet suddenly were under me no more, the dirt was in my face, and something that felt like a slab of granite was on my back. I heard a shout, the roar of a shot, then felt a great throbbing explosion in my skull. The weight left my back; I rolled to the side, head spinning.

"Fiddler! Fiddler, where are you?"

My eyes were open, yet saw nothing but vague shapes and light. Whatever had struck me had dazed me worse even than that befuddled Mennonite propped up against the wagon wheel. Gripping the back of my head, I felt blood.

He must have dropped on me from above; Big Jim had probably hidden on the stable roof, waiting for us to get into just the right position. I was grateful he hadn't snapped my spine. Who had fired the shot I heard? I had been in no position to tell; all I had heard was an indistinct roar that might have been Fiddler's shotgun, or Big Jim's pistol firing close to my ears. The echo of it still rattled around inside my skull.

More gunfire, from around the corner. I groped for my pistol . . . gone. Big Jim must have swept it from my holster. My rifle was gone, too.

I was unarmed in a town occupied only by shadows and two other men, each determined to kill the other.

Part of me wanted to run as hard as I could, to get on my horse and ride out—for if Fiddler Smith died here, Big Jim would come for me. The thought of being hunted among this gathering of empty buildings, hunted like a mouse by a cat, was more terrifying than any nightmare. I would circle around to the horses, mount, and get out.

No . . . no. I couldn't do that, not and leave Fiddler here alone. That would be a coward's way. Somehow I had to help Fiddler—but with no weapon, how could I do it?

Again there was a burst of gunfire, farther away. The last blast was unmistakably that of Fiddler's shotgun, followed by silence. I grinned. Fiddler had gotten him! But immediately two pistol shots resounded, and I heard a scream.

Fiddler's scream.

I darted onto the street. Where were they? "Fiddler!" I yelled, "Fiddler, are you alive?"

Onto the street he stepped, coming from the far side of one of the empty houses. He grinned, smoking pistol still in hand. His scarred face was all the more fearsome for his smile.

"Now it's your turn, McCan," Big Jim said. "Now you'll die like Fiddler died."

"I have no weapon," I said, backing away. "You can't shoot me unarmed."

"I can't? Then tell me how it is I can do this!" He fired the pistol; my left leg buckled beneath me and blood streamed down my thigh.

"You're a coward, Big Jim!" I yelled. "Only a coward would gun down a man who's got no chance to fight back!"

"For that I'll cut out your tongue, before I give you the chance to die," he said, lifting the pistol again.

The shot echoed among the buildings. I had closed my eyes instinctively, and when I opened them again, what remained of Big Jim's head was not anything I wanted to look at long. Fiddler's shotgun blast had taken him right in the side of the head, striking him, ironically, on his single good ear. The results you can probably imagine without me spelling them out.

"Well, now it really is done," Fiddler said as the shotgun fell from his fingers. He slumped down to his knees, then leaned to the side. Blood poured from a hole in his chest.

I pushed myself up on my bleeding, numb leg.

To my surprise I was able to stand; the wound was grazing and superficial, nicking a vein and numbing a nerve, but doing little beyond that. I went to Fiddler's side.

"I'm thinking I might need some help, McCan," he said weakly.

"Can you ride?"

"I got my doubts."

Panic was beginning to well; inspiration, fortunately, overtook it. "Bund! I'll go back to Bund and bring that wagon up, then we can ride you to help. Fiddler, I'm going to get you into this building here and cover you up . . . you rest until I get back with Bund's wagon—you understand?"

"Don't think . . . I'll be dancing any jigs . . . while I wait . . ." I could hear the hurting in his voice.

"It's going to be all right, Fiddler. I promise you, everything's going to be all right."

"He's dead, isn't he . . ."

"He's dead. Big Jim can't bother you anymore."

"Not until . . . I meet him on the other side . . . likely we'll be in the same place, me and him . . ."

"Shut up and lie down. I'll be back, fast as I can."

I made him as comfortable as I could, then limped across to the horses, and rode out.

Epilogue

Longhurst inhaled what looked like a palmful of snuff, sneezed, and wiped his nose with a handkerchief. We were in the front room of our house, me with my bandaged leg propped up on a stool. I touched the sore place gingerly with my stiffened hand, thinking how my adventures with Fiddler Smith had left their marks on my physical person. My inner person, too—I wouldn't be quite the same again, having known him.

"Now, wait a minute," Longhurst said. "Let me understand this. You rode out of New Hazelton and found this Mennonite fellow again, and when you got back on the wagon, Fiddler was gone?"

"Vanished like a ghost. There was Big Jim's corpse, just as before, but Fiddler was gone. His horse, too. Yet he couldn't have ridden out—he was in no shape for it. The only thing I can figure is that someone came along and found him during the time I was gone, and took him away, and his horse with him."

"Took him away—dead or alive?"

"I like to think the latter. I'm inclined more to believe the former."

"It's a sad thing," Maggie said, holding Martha on her lap and looking at her as if she feared she would vanish before her eyes. Since Longhurst had safely brought the child home, Maggie had been like that with her, doting and loving and clinging to her every moment. "His life seemed so . . . wasted, I guess."

"He held the same view himself," I replied. "As for me, I'm not going to judge him. He had good in him and bad. We're all that way, just with different mixes."

"I still can't figure it, him vanishing like he did," Longhurst said. "It's surely a mystery. And why, McCan, if somebody came along and hauled off his corpse like you think, didn't they haul off Big Jim's corpse too?"

For that I had no answer; it was a point well made. Even so, I remained sure my partner from Walden City was dead; I felt it more than knew it.

Fiddler was gone, and with him the trouble that always came along with him. Life could now become what I wanted it to be—Maggie and Martha and I, at home, at work, and at peace.

But before the peace would come the tears, and that night I shed them. Tears of grief for two shortened and tragic lives: those of Fiddler Smith and Vera Ann Walden.

Longhurst and Miss Flatt were married in the summer in a flamboyant ceremony and reception the likes of which the Emporium hadn't seen since Maggie's marriage to Rodney Upchurch. By now Miss Flatt—who after the wedding proudly informed us we could feel free to call her . . . no, not Ambrosia, but Mrs. Longhurst—was twice the

weight she had been when we hired her. Longhurst
had his own name for her—Fats. The funny thing
was, she didn't seem to mind it.

The L&M thrived and grew, and over the years
Longhurst actually became a good cattleman. The
Emporium also thrived—but the best thriving was
done by little Martha, who turned from a chubby
baby to one of the prettiest little girls I had ever
seen. In time she gained playmates, children born
to Maggie and me, all of them dark-haired like their
parents. Martha stood out; her hair was shining
gold.

The mystery of Fiddler's disappearance was
never solved. In fact, the mystery only deepened.
Two years after that final shoot-out in the empty
Mennonite settlement, an envelope addressed to
Martha McCan showed up in the mail. Inside was
two dollars. No note, no marks to indicate who had
sent it, or why. Three months later another envelope came, only a dollar inside this time. From then
on such mystery gifts arrived at irregular intervals,
containing varying small amounts of cash. All were
addressed to Martha, the name and address crudely
scrawled.

"It's Fiddler," Maggie would say. "It's his way
of trying to do something good for the daughter of
the girl he loved."

"Fiddler's dead, Maggie," I would reply. "I
know he's dead."

"You don't know it," she countered. "You just
think you do."

And perhaps she was right, for one autumn evening in Sheridan, Wyoming, a long time after, the
year of 1897, there happened an incident that left
me wondering.

I was there on business, having traveled alone. The business finished, I was on my way back to the hotel, when I passed the open door of a saloon. Nothing about the place caught my attention and I gave it not a glance as I swept by . . . and then I heard it. Music. Sweet, high-toned fiddle music played in a flourishing style that was as familiar as this morning yet as distant as memory.

I froze at the saloon doorway, staring straight ahead. The music bubbled out, pulling from my mind a voice singing the words of this very tune: "Love somebody and I do I do, love somebody and I do . . ."

For several seconds I remained where I was, still looking ahead. One glance inside would have answered the question. I started to turn my head . . .

Then I bolted forward, having never looked. The music faded behind me. When I reached my hotel room my heart was racing.

I was glad I hadn't looked. There are some mysteries best left unsolved, some questions best left unanswered, and some memories best left as memories, and nothing more.

Author's Note

Renegade Lawmen is a work of fiction, but makes reference to some historical places and events, a few of which are worthy of note. There really was a mining town named Craig City in Colorado, and the Independent Army described in this novel did operate there, did collect Indian ears for bounty, and was substantially wiped out in a responding Sioux massacre. There never was a Fiddler Smith in the Independent Army, however; he, like McCan, is a fictitious character.

Walden City is also fictional; I have located it approximately in the area actually occupied at the time by the gold-mining town of Manhattan, about forty miles west of Fort Collins.

The settlement of Upchurch, Montana, is a fictional community I introduced in the novel *Timber Creek*, which tells Luke McCan's story prior to the period of *Renegade Lawmen*. New Hazelton is also a fictional community. Miles City, Powderville, Glendive, and Bozeman are among the actual Montana locales mentioned in the book.

Lastly, the train accident in Chatsworth, Illinois, to which the death of McCan's fiancée is attributed in the novel, actually occurred as described. It took the lives of a hundred people and injured many more, and was considered one of the worst such accidents of its time.

CAMERON JUDD
April 2, 1991